MINDBLIND

JENNIFER ROY

MARSHALL CAVENDISH

Copyright © 2010 by Jennifer Roy
All rights reserved
No part of this publication may be reproduced, stored in a retrieval system or transmitted, in any form or by any means, electronic, mechanical, photocopying, recording, or otherwise, without the prior permission of the copyright owner. Request for permission should be addressed to the Publisher, Marshall Cavendish Corporation, 99 White Plains Road, Tarrytown, NY 10591. Tel: (914) 332-8888, fax: (914) 332-1888.

Web site: www.marshallcavendish.us/kids

This book is a work of fiction. Names, characters, places, and incidents are products of the author's imagination and are used fictitiously. Any resemblance to actual events or locales or persons, living or dead, is entirely coincidental.

Other Marshall Cavendish Offices:

Marshall Cavendish International (Asia) Private Limited, 1 New Industrial Road, Singapore 536196 • Marshall Cavendish International (Thailand) Co Ltd. 253 Asoke, 12th Flr, Sukhumvit 21 Road, Klongtoey Nua, Wattana, Bangkok 10110, Thailand • Marshall Cavendish (Malaysia) Sdn Bhd, Times Subang, Lot 46, Subang Hi-Tech Industrial Park, Batu Tiga, 40000 Shah Alam, Selangor Darul Ehsan, Malaysia

Marshall Cavendish is a trademark of Times Publishing Limited

Library of Congress Cataloging-in-Publication Data

Roy, Jennifer Rozines, 1967-
Mindblind / Jennifer Roy. – 1st ed.
p. cm.
Summary: Fourteen-year-old Nathaniel Clark, who has Asperger's Syndrome, tries to prove that he is a genius so that he can become a member of the prestigious Aldus Institute, the premier organization for the profoundly gifted.
ISBN 978-0-7614-5716-9
[1. Asperger's syndrome–Fiction. 2. Genius–Fiction. 3. Rock groups–Fiction. 4. Interpersonal relations–Fiction.] I. Title.
PZ7.R812185Mi 2011
[Fic]–dc22
2010006966

Book design by Alex Ferrari
Editor: Margery Cuyler

Printed in China (E)
First edition
10 9 8 7 6 5 4 3 2 1

Marshall Cavendish

To Gregory,
a wonderful, supportive husband and father

Open File: C:\My Files\genius\first_time.avi (Date: 1/14/99)

I am three years old. At the doctor's office. The nurse is testing my eyesight. She holds up a picture of a furry, red monster.

"What do you see?" she asks me.

I stare at a point just over her right shoulder and reply, "If your child is experiencing at least three of the following symptoms, ask your physician if Zendoxin might be right for her."

The nurse does not move. My mother gets up from the chair on which she's been sitting and plucks one of the pamphlets off a counter display. She hands it to the nurse.

"Did your boy just *read* this?" The nurse stares at the pamphlet, then at me.

The furry, red monster is now lying on the counter, forgotten.

"I guess his vision is all right," my mother says.

The doctor walks into the room.

"Seems like you have a little genius (File: genius) here," the nurse says.

5

"Really?" The doctor kneels down and puts his face near mine. "What's our genius's name?"

I am inspecting a piece of thread that is hanging off my pants.

"What is your name?" the doctor asks again. His words create a blast of coffee-scented air in my face.

I really dislike the smell of coffee.

"Elmo," I say. "*E-L-M-O.*"

"Honey, tell him your real name," my mother prompts.

I turn my head away from the doctor and mumble, "Nathaniel."

"A bit louder this time," Dr. Coffeemouth says. "What is your name?"

"Nathaniel Gideon Clark!" I yell. "The surgeon general warns that more than two cups of coffee per day may be hazardous to the fetus in women who are pregnant!"

"Oh. Kay." The doctor stands up. "Nathaniel's lungs sound good. Now how about we take a look at the rest of him?"

While the doctor examines me, I go into my head files and create a new folder. I name it "jeenyes" and store images of the nurse who first said that new word.

Close File.

Later I rename the folder "genius."

Open File: C:\My Files\genius\second_time.avi (Date: 2/22/99)

"What is he, some kind of genius?" the cashier at the checkout asks. I've been watching the items pass over the moving belt. *Beep* apples. *Beep* paper towels. Last item, *beep* magazine.

"Thirty-three dollars and ten cents," I announce.

The cashier says, "He's right. That's the subtotal. What is he, some kind of genius?"

She pushes a few keys and then tells my father, "That's thirty-five forty-one."

WHAT???

"No! No! No!" I start to cry.

"Stop it, Nathaniel," my father hisses. "Behave."

But I'm inconsolable and have to be dragged out of the store.

Back at home my mother explains about sales tax, and I calm down. The world makes sense when numbers add up.

Close File.

Subtotal plus sales tax equals total. Subtotal plus sales tax equals total. Subtotal plus sales tax equals total. Subtotal plus sales tax equals total. It looped around my brain for days, until I shortened it.

s + St = T

I realized back then that making formulas for things relaxed me. I began carrying around a spiral notebook and writing formulas in it to explain the world around me.

$s + St = T$ was my first written expression. As the world become more confusing, my note*book* became note*books*, and my formulas became like friends.

CHAPTER ONE
ACTIVATE SHIELDS

"**H**ey, Genius," Braden Sheehan says. "Pass me those chips, willya?"

I pick up the bag of potato chips and lob it from my chair to the couch where Braden sits. The bag flies over Braden's head, hits the wall, and drops with a *crunch-thud* behind the couch.

"G-man, you killed the chips." Braden groans as he lifts his bulky football-player body and looks down into the space between the wall and couch.

"Leave them," my best friend, Cooper, says. "We've got more."

Cooper presses Pause on his controller, and the action on the wide-screen TV freezes. "I'll go get 'em. Be right back." Cooper leaves.

"Sorry," I say to Braden.

"Yeah, just don't go out for the football team." Braden snorts. He knows I wouldn't. I don't do teams or sports.

But I do play Whirled Domination 2 really well, which is likely the reason Braden tolerates my presence.

Cooper comes back into the entertainment room. He gives Braden the chips and an energy drink and hands me a bottled water, with the cap already off.

Cooper and I have been neighbors for ten years and nine months. Since we were both four. He's one month older. While his family was building the mini-mansion on the lot next door, I was miserable. The construction sounds were agony to my super-sensitive ears. But then the noise stopped and a moving van pulled into the newly paved driveway, followed by a white Range Rover.

Open File: C:\My Files\range_rover.avi (Date: 2/12/00)

White Range Rover. License plate California 2ACX555. A boy jumps out and looks across the lawn at me. He has brown hair and a superhero cape.

"I'm Superman!" the kid says. "You want to be Batman or Spider-Man?"

"I want to be Nathaniel," I inform him; and he runs into his new house, cape flapping behind him.

Close File.

That was the first time I met Cooper Owens. Once he got used to me, he decided we were friends. Cooper's gotten me to push my limits—such as inviting me to join his garage band, making me try snowboarding, and even including me on a couple of group dates. He's an applied force putting pressure on me.

$P = F \div A$

(Where P is pressure, F is force, and A is applied area.)

Because of Cooper, I have had some semblance of a social life over the past decade. Not that I'd ever asked for one.

"Die! Die! Dumb sucker!" Braden is back playing the video game, warring with enemy man-boars. The man-boars surround his character, baring their sharp teeth. Braden's avatar is about to be shredded and devoured.

"Nathaniel?" Cooper says.

"Braden, push the X and left arrow," I say. "Good. Now hit Fire and Up simultaneously."

A burst of red light comes out of Braden's weapon. It shoots up in the air and explodes like a fireworks display.

"Activate shields," I instruct Braden. I watch the screen as red flames rain down to the ground, frying all the man-boars. Braden's human, protected by his shields, is unscathed.

"Awesome," says Braden. "Pig roast."

Cooper and Braden do a "cheers" with their energy drinks. I tip my bottle up for a drink, but I somehow miss my mouth and dribble water down the front of my shirt.

"Uh." I stand and set down the 8-ounce minus 2-ounces water bottle. The wetness of the shirt makes my skin feel slimy. I have to go home and change out of it immediately.

"I'm going," I say. "I'm in the middle of a paper on how the sustainability movement can improve Asia's political stature without diminishing its economic growth. And I'm writing it in Mandarin Chinese because I might be able to get it published in an Asian economic journal. Or newspaper, at least."

I stop. I've been talking way too much.

"Sorry," I say to Braden and Cooper. "Good-bye."

"See you tomorrow at band practice, Nathaniel," Cooper says.

"Later, G." Braden grunts.

I'm two-thirds down the hallway, heading for the door, when I hear Braden.

"Dang. That kid is like half genius, half retard."

$(N = \frac{1}{2}G + \frac{1}{2}r)$

I mentally activate my personal shield. No words or negativity can penetrate it.

I keep walking, let myself out, and shut the door

behind me. I don't wait to hear Cooper's response.

N + C/B = ERROR, where N = Nathaniel, C = Cooper, B = Braden

Open File: C:\My Files\genius\retarded.avi (Date: 5/15/03)

"If he's such a genius, why can't he tie his own shoes?" my father says. I am in the kitchen eating a warm chocolate chip cookie my mother just baked and reading a book. My parents are in the living room, where I can hear every word.

"I'm the only father bending down to lace his seven-year-old's cleats. And he ran the wrong way three times today. Three! After I told him the first two times where the other team's goal was, he does it again?"

"Steven, calm down," my mother says.

"So I hear a parent on the other team ask if he is retarded." My father's voice is not getting calmer. "What am I supposed to do? Say, 'No. Actually, ma'am, my son's IQ is more than yours and your son's— who scored three goals and ties his own shoes—put together?' I'd sound like a g.d. lunatic!"

My cookie does not taste as good as it did two minutes ago.

"Steven, if you'd just come with me to the psychologist, he can explain Nathaniel's behaviors," says my mother.

"I do not need some stranger spouting feel-good mumbo jumbo to tell me about my own son. Look. He is seven years old. Stop babying him, and he won't be such a baby," my father says. "Therapy session over."

I can hear my mother start to cry. This makes me feel dizzy. I don't want my mother to cry.

"That kid should be able to figure out this stuff," my father grumbles, "if he's such a genius."

I walk into the living room.

"Technically," I say, "I'm not a genius."

I hold up the book I've been reading: *Help! My Child Is Gifted!* I'd taken it off my mother's library pile.

"It says in here," I tell my father, "that a genius is a person who has accomplished something outstanding with his or her talents."

My mother stops crying. I go over to her and put my arms around her. (She taught me how to hug, but I do not like the squeezing, so I just do the arms part. This is called empathy, and I have been practicing.)

My father is looking at us.

"I haven't done anything exceptional that makes an impact on the world," I say. "So I am not a genius."

"You've got chocolate all over your face." My father shakes his head. "You look like an idiot. Maybe at your next therapy session they can teach you how to use a napkin."

He stomps out of the room.

My mother kisses the top of my head.

"Nathaniel," she says, "you accomplish great things every day just by being you."

I make my arms squeeze my mom.

Then it hits me.

I'm not a genius?

I flip open the book to where I'd left off.

The word 'genius' is loaded with different meanings and connotations," I read to myself. *"But many experts prefer not to call a person a genius until he or she has accomplished something outstanding. Einstein, Newton, Curie, Gates . . . all earned the title 'genius' because of their significant contributions to the world, not because of their IQs Therefore it is best not to pressure children early with labels they may— or may not—be able to live up to.*

I have an extremely high IQ of 182. But apparently I am not a genius yet.

In order to be labeled a genius, I must make a contribution to the world. I can do that. I will start, right after I wash the chocolate off my face. If I want to be seen as a genius, I should not look like an idiot.

Close File.

Open File: C:\My Files\labels.avi (Date: 3/19/04)

"Labels are just words," my mother says. We've recently seen a new doctor who has given me yet another diagnosis. "They don't tell you who you are."

"Yes, they do," I correct her. I'm in my electronic-label-maker phase, fascinated by the different fonts and symbols.

I show my mother the NATHANIEL GIDEON CLARK labels on my watchband, my belt, and the inner flaps of my sneakers.

"See? My labels tell me who I am."

"Hmmm . . . ," my mother says. "They sure do."

Close File.

CHAPTER TWO

SLAM INTO THE WALL OF REALITY

I am in my bedroom. I changed out of my wet shirt and feel more comfortable. Actually, my bedroom is the only place in the world where I can feel totally comfortable. I am aware that teenagers are supposed to enjoy "hanging out" with their agemates. But the only teenager I really want to hang out with is myself.

I became an official teenager twenty months ago, so now I am fourteen and two-thirds. Fourteen is a very *un*interesting number. Now, sixteen— that is a good one. At sixteen you can get your driver's permit, *and* you become a double numeric digit in hexadecimal.

But fourteen has not been an auspicious age in the life of Nathaniel Clark. For example, have *you* heard of me? No? Exactly. Because I have not become a genius.

Yet. Horrifyingly, at age fourteen the equation remains: $N \neq G$: Nathaniel does not equal genius.

The final nail on my genius coffin was hammered in last year on July 15, 2009. My mother and I flew on an airplane to Denver, Colorado, for an interview at the Aldus Institute.

I had sent in my application and had made the final cut. Now all that was left was the personal interview and then I would be accepted into the premier organization for the profoundly gifted.

Or so I'd thought.

Open File: C:\My Files\genius\Aldus.avi (Date: 7/15/09)

"Nathaniel, your aptitudes and evaluations are quite impressive," Jane-the-admissions-head said.

"Yes," I agreed. My mother tapped my hand—our signal for *manners*.

"Thank you," I added.

"However . . . ," Jane said. *However?* my mind buzzed. *However what? However did you get so smart?*

"However, we are concerned that your level of accomplishment may not be up to our standards here at the Aldus," Jane said.

Calm. Stay calm.

"Perhaps you are missing some pertinent information?" I say, reaching into my briefcase and pulling out a copy of my personal bio. I share it with interested parties so I do not have to repeat myself.

Nathaniel Gideon Clark
Age 13
Currently a senior at University of Arizona Distance Learning.
Bachelor of Science in Computer Science with double minor in
Mandarin Chinese and Mathematics, expected May 2010.

Graduated Distance-Learning High School at Age 11 in June 2007, GPA: 4.2

Scored 5 on AP exams—Calculus, Physics, Economics, Mandarin
SAT scores: 800 / 800 / 800 (2008)
720 / 800 / 580 (2005)—Youth Talent Search; ELA, Mathematics, Writing

COMPETITIONS:
   Mathematics:
      USAMO qualifier—39/42, black mop (2008)
      AIME—14/15 (2008)
      AMC 12—150 points (perfect score, 2008)
   Future City Competition
      Team took second place in state finals (2005, 2006)

Business owner, Nathaniel's Fair Trade Organic Coffee ($1,200 profit, 2008)

Hobbies: geography, keyboardist in music group, bowling

"Yes," Jane says. "We received this with your applications. It's very nice, but it left the committee with some unanswered questions. For example, you made it so far in the math competitions, yet you did not go to Romania for the Internationals, where you could have proven yourself globally. Why didn't you go?"

Because my father forgot to send in the paperwork by the deadline although he had insisted he had done it, and both *my parents had to sign and submit it, so I was declared ineligible . . . .*

I could not speak. Jane continued.

"And your essay to us describes geography in great detail, yet you never entered a geography bee. And has your band been signed by a record label—major or independent?"

I shook my head *no* to the second question. I had thought the answer to the first was obvious. Geography was a passionate interest; why would I suck the fun out of it by sitting on a chair for hours and hours, occasionally rising to answer one question and then going back to waiting? (I am not good at waiting.)

"You have gifts, certainly," Jane said, "but we'd like to see what you have *achieved* with them."

"Uh." My mother cleared her throat. She was supposed to stay silent in the silent-parent's chair, but she could see I was floundering.

"Nathaniel will be a magna cum laude college graduate when he's fourteen," my mother reiterated.

"That's wonderful," Jane agreed, "but what are Nathaniel's plans after that? "Currently we have on our roster a pipe-organ prodigy who has performed for the pope, a student who has coauthored numerous scientific journal articles, and a visionary artist who sold out her first gallery show at the age of eleven. I could go on, but suffice it to say that our students are so devoted to their gifts that they live and breathe them with single-minded determination."

"So, what you are saying is that Nathaniel is *too* well-rounded?" My mother stood up.

Uh-oh. This was not heading in the right direction.

"Well," Jane said calmly, "multipotentiality is just that: the potential to succeed in multiple areas. We'd like to see Nathaniel's potential become more focused and lead to a tangible result."

"All these years we've worked to make him a whole person and not just an obsessive robot," my mother muttered, shaking her head.

As for me, I was feeling vertigo, nausea, and the overwhelming urge to chew off all my fingernails. I started with my thumbnail.

Jane ushered us out of the room before I completely lost it. As the door shut behind us, I looked at my mom and ripped my thumbnail clear off.

"Genius denied," I said. And the familiar loop began playing in my head: $N \neq G$. $N \neq G$.

$N = $ zero

Close File.

CHAPTER THREE
PUT ON MY FEELINGS FACE

It's 8:00 p.m. I shake off the horrid memory of that visit. Back to the present. I've scheduled a Skype call with my friend Molly. I turn on the computer, connect to Skype, and wait for Molly.

I met Molly on October 13, 2005, at a group for kids with Asperger's syndrome. Usually, I do not like to socialize with other Asperger's kids. We are all too self-absorbed. But Molly and I got along and have stayed friends.

Ass Burger.

That's what people (mostly under the age of eighteen) call Asperger's syndrome when they think they are being funny. They are not. It's named after a guy named Hans Asperger. Sometimes people shorten it to AS or Aspie.

Open File: C:\My Files\Asperger's syndrome\description.jpg
From the *Asperger's Syndrome Manual*, Volume 2:
People with AS have:
trouble with social skills
communicative difficulties
obsessive interests and rigid thinking
sensory sensitivities
clumsy or stiff movement
Names people with AS are called:
eccentric, quirky, loner, nerd, genius, geek, Spocklike, weird
Close File.

AS is NOT a mental illness or a disease, but it does affect the brain and body. There are many ways to treat the symptoms of Asperger's. Personally, I have had my brain, blood, poop, and urine tested. I have been on special diets, taken vitamins, and done a zillion therapies. Totally humiliating, occasionally helpful.

All of those therapies, plus my mom's support, have made my outward behaviors and personality more socially acceptable. My AS is now considered "mild." But it is still there. I am not cured. I don't want to be. Maybe some people want their AS to disappear so they can be like everyone else, but not me. I like being the way I am.

It is the neurotypical (regular-brained) world that wants to fix me. And the reality is, their world is the world I have to live in, so I have spent years training to function in it. And now the "experts" are thinking of getting rid of the Asperger's diagnosis altogether. (They want to say we are high-functioning autistics!) Well, I continue to say Asperger's.

One of the Asperger's traits is "resistance to dealing with change." So, I'm not changing anything. Asperger's it is.

A lot of famous people probably had Asperger's syndrome. Thomas Jefferson, Albert Einstein, Marie Curie, and Charles M. Schultz. People think Bill Gates has it, too.

So I'm not alone.

Oops. I'm not alone. Molly has shown up. Her face fills the screen.

"Hi, Nathaniel," she says.

"Hi, Molly," I say.

"I made this picture," she says. She holds up a drawing in front of the webcam. It is of a horse. As always.

"Awesome," I say. "Your intricate details and exact proportions make it seem lifelike." I read that statement in an art review in *TIME* magazine.

"Yeah," she says.

"So this horse retired from racing on January

twenty-second, and you can see his strong leg muscles," Molly says, pointing to her picture.

"Wow," I say. "I have decided I need to become a genius as soon as possible."

Molly is silent for twelve seconds.

"Aren't you already a genius?" she asks.

"Technically, I am not a genius," I say. "Until I have made a significant contribution to the world. I have to harness my talents to make an impact."

"You said *harness*." Molly giggles. I knew she'd get my joke.

"I need to come up with a plan to become an official genius," I announce.

"Does it involve horses?" Molly asks excitedly.

"Er, I don't know, maybe," I say. If there was a possibility for equestrian involvement, I knew Molly would stay interested.

"Cool!" Molly smiles. Cooper says that Molly is cute, with her brown curly hair and olivey skin. Her father is Jordanian and her mother is a dance instructor.

"So, what I'm thinking . . . ," I begin.

"Oops, I must go," Molly says abruptly. "See you Saturday."

Her face disappears.

I go bowling with Molly on Saturdays from 12:00

noon until 2:00 p.m. It is not a romantic date. We both just like bowling.

$B = F_h$, where B = Bowling

F sub h means "a happy feeling." I have had a WHAT ARE YOU FEELING? poster taped to the wall of my bedroom since I was small. I was supposed to learn to recognize and identify which feeling face described me. But I didn't want all those faces staring at me in bed, so I *X*'d each one out. Then I wrote a feelings symbol for each. F_a = angry, F_f = frustrated, and so on. The ones I've most identified with over the years are F_c = confused, F_f, and F_h. I consider myself a basically happy guy (even if I forget to "show" it by smiling).

Does it surprise you that I have friends?

Contrary to what some people believe, people with Asperger's are not robots without emotions. I have feelings; I just may not express them like other people. I like my friends Molly and Cooper who are my own age, and I like my friends who are adults. I love my mother intensely. And my grandmother, who lives 2,497 miles away in Phoenix, Arizona.

I am also in love with a girl named Jessa. She does not know it.

Okay. That was way more cogitating about people and my feelings about people than I am used to doing.

Time to go back to my comfort zone: the computer.

I pull up my sustainability article. I am almost finished. I have a program that allows me to use Chinese characters. Did you know that the Chinese language requires the use of double the binary digits in computing? I do my best not to lose anything in the translation, which leads me to perfectionist thinking. But before I go totally OCD, I back off and finish the article.

I send it out to an online Chinese-American newspaper, a West-friendly newspaper in Hong Kong, and shoot one out to my e-mail buddy Wen, who is a blogger in Tai Pei. I also decide to e-mail it to the U.S. ambassador to China.

China has been one of my special interests since I was four. I told my parents I wanted to learn Chinese. Apparently that was an unusual request, as we are not Chinese.

After repeating my request every day for weeks, I began formal lessons via a computer program. Informally, I learned even more at my mother's weekly manicure appointment.

Open File: C:\My Files\Mandarin Chinese\manicure.avi (Date: 6/11/00)

"Well, I'm embarrassed," my mother says as we are driving home from the nail salon. Her freshly painted fingernails look very glossy against the dark steering wheel. I can smell them

from my booster seat in the back.

"I just *assumed* they were Korean," she continues. "Is that prejudice? I thought all nail salons were run by Koreans!"

I had been listening to the chatter among the employees. I bravely, haltingly, asked Nancy (it said on her tag) in Chinese what time it was. Nancy responded that it was 2:30.

Then Nancy stopped buffing my mother's nails. Soon all the employees had gathered around me. They applauded as I counted to twenty in Mandarin (being careful to pronounce the tricky *four* correctly). Then I lost my shyness and belted out, "Head, shoulders, knees, and toes;" and all the technicians tried to keep up with me as I tapped each body part.

None of the customers, including my mother, could participate due to their fingers and/or toes being in various stages of manipedi.

When we were finished, we said our *dzye zaijians* (good-byes). As the door closed behind me, a bell jingled and I heard Nancy say in Mandarin, "A yellow-haired, blue-eyed American boy learning Chinese?" Then in English, "What he thinking?"

Close File.

A famous Aspie on the autistic spectrum named Temple Grandin says she "thinks in pictures." That made me consider my own thinking. I've concluded that my brain is equivalent to a computer. Superfast processing speed, tremendous capacity for storage and retrieval, with occasional glitches and meltdowns.

All my memories are named, filed, and saved. I can call them up when I need them (e.g., an image of a textbook for a test). My photographic memory is like a digital camera that automatically uploads into my system. It is very convenient.

Except when it's not. I will be talking to someone or reading or concentrating on something when a word triggers a memory and up pops a file. Then the image distracts me or the movie-memory plays, and I have to watch until it ends. I have no Stop or Escape. And there's no Delete. Every millisecond of my life is in there.

This has caused people to wonder if I have ADD or seizures, or if I'm just ignoring them.

Cooper says I look like a zombie when it happens. Molly doesn't notice. My father has tried all sorts of tricks: snapping his fingers in my face, yelling (big surprise), trying to shame me out of it by calling me names that imply intellectual deficiency. My mother just waits. Sometimes she asks what movie I've been watching. I tell her about the good ones.

So I have files in my head and formulas down on paper. A lot of material to utilize in my quest for genius.

"Nathaniel!" My mother knocks on the door. I'm now playing Minesweeper on my computer. Mom comes in.

"Your father's on the phone." She hands me the cordless and leaves. It's difficult for me to stop what I'm doing (good) and do something I don't want to do (Dad). It makes me go Aspie.

I put the phone to my ear.

"Did you know that a group of hippos is called a *bloat* of hippopotami?" I say.

"Hi, Nathaniel," my father's voice booms out, so I hold the phone away from my ear. "No, I didn't know that. Hippos. Huh."

The hippopotamus factoid had popped into my head when I thought of my father, who has gained quite a bit of weight since he remarried. His new wife cooks all his favorite foods.

"Anyway," my father continues, "I called to see what's up. What are you up to?"

"I've been working on an essay regarding motivational strategies to encourage the sustainability movement in China."

"Great, great," my father says. "Is this a paper for school?"

"No."

"Okay, well . . ." I hear my father's wife's voice in the background. "I've got to go, Champ. I'll see you Saturday usual time, right?"

"See you Saturday, right, okay," I say, and click off.

What to do now? My computer's clock says 10:12 p.m. I swivel my chair, stretch, and look out my window. I can see directly into Cooper's bedroom. When the light is on. But his light is off. It is Thursday, a school night, so I can't call over there. I'm homeschooled, so my schedule is not so rigid.

I swivel back to my computer, log onto the private Web site for the Robinson Institute—minimum IQ 160—and lurk around. There are always users on this site at night. Profoundly gifted people are often insomniacs. I join in on a group called WWWBD? (What Would Warren Buffett Do?) and settle in for a stimulating night.

CHAPTER FOUR

ZERO IS THE HERO (SOMETIMES)

The next day I'm back at Cooper's, the way I always am on Fridays from 4:00 p.m. to 7:00 p.m., for band practice.

"And that's the way it should be," Jessa Rose is singing, "because I know you will be there for me."

I play the last few chords on my keyboard, Cooper's guitar fades out, and Logan Finley holds up his drumsticks.

For a moment there is silence. Then, "Oh yeah!" Cooper says. "That rocked! We rock! Jess, you're a rock goddess!"

"Thank you, thank you." Jessa turns toward us and does a little bow. She clicks off her microphone, and we all shut down our instruments.

I pull out my earplugs and stick them in my jeans

pocket. I can still hear the music when they're in; they just lower the intensity that offends my auditory sensitivity.

"Okay, guys," Jessa says, "time to talk business."

It is hard for me to concentrate on Jessa's words. She is so pretty, it is distracting. When we're playing, I'm all into the music; but when we're not, I'm all into Jessa.

"So we have only three weeks until my cousin Claudia's bat mitzvah," Jessa says. "I made each of you a copy of the set list."

"Our second professional gig already. Cooper grins. "One hundred more George Washingtons."

"Divided by four," I remind him. "Twenty-five for each of us." I happen to know Cooper gets one hundred dollars a week for allowance, so he's not in the band for financial gain.

"Works for me," Logan mumbles from behind his drum set. That's about three more words than he usually says. Logan is overweight, with shaggy red hair that flies all over when he's banging the drums. He's really good; he drums so fast his hair and drumsticks blur. Cooper recruited him from the school marching band.

"Money, music, and women," Cooper says. "That's what a rock band is all about."

Jessa whacks him on the head with her set list papers.

"Those 'women' will be thirteen years old," she says. "It's a bat mitzvah, not a bachelorette party."

Sometimes I can't believe a girl like Jessa would put up with us. Then I look around at the garage Cooper's father converted into a music studio, and I know why. High-quality equipment. Great acoustics. Temperature control. All because Cooper decided he wanted to be in a band.

Open File: C:\My Files\band\first time.avi (Date: 7/21/06)

"We need to start a band," Cooper says. We are in my family room playing Risk. Of course I'm winning, but Cooper likes playing anyway, because he makes theatrical death scenes for his soldiers. I've just wiped out his artillery in Europe, and he has been rolling around on the floor making dying sounds. Until he popped up and announced the band thing.

"We do?" I do not know if Cooper is being serious. Occasionally he is.

"We do," Cooper echoes emphatically. "Bands are very cool. We can call ourselves The Cooper Owens Band."

"You don't even play an instrument," I point out.

"I can learn," Cooper says. He starts rocking his head forward and back really fast and moving his fingers in a strange way.

"Are you autistic too?" I ask, suddenly excited. "Because I have Asperger's, which is in the high-functioning range of the autistic spectrum; and when I get excited, I do finger motions, too—"

"I'm playing air guitar, doofus," Cooper interrupts. I squint. There is air, but definitely no guitar.

Close File.

Whatever Cooper wants, his parents give him. So back then it was Cooper on guitar and me on keyboard making lots of noise. But gradually we got better, and the garage and the garage band became a reality.

"Hey!" Cooper's shout snaps me out of my memory. "What the *H* is this?"

Jessa hands me a sheet of paper. Cooper and Logan already have theirs. I read:

Band Name: ?

Event: Claudia Rose's Bat Mitzvah

Date: October 20

And then I see the four songs we've been rehearsing. We're the opening band. They have also hired a deejay.

"I thought we could use a new name," Jessa says calmly. "Since we're now a successful *group*." It's true. We were a big success at Jessa's older sister Jade's sweet sixteen party. Jade said we rocked, as her friends were dancing and singing along with us.

"The Cooper Owens Band is a great name," Cooper howls. "It's a hostile takeover! Troops, back me up!"

He looks at me. *Uh, what?*

"It's *my* garage." Cooper crosses his arms and glares at Jessa. Jessa walks up to him. Cooper, at five foot eleven, is seven and a half inches taller than Jessa. He's also muscley from the weight room his football team uses.

I watch Jessa. She is smallish, with dark, almost black hair and brown eyes with thick eyelashes. When she looks at me, I feel funny.

Right now, she's looking up at Cooper.

"It's *my* voice," she says. "And my cousin."

"Okay, okay," Cooper says. "New name. Anyone?"

We're all quiet.

"Three Rock Stars and a Zero?" says Logan.

"What does that mean?" Jessa asks.

Logan is still sitting behind his drums. "You know." He shrugs. "You're *American Idol* winner twenty twelve; Cooper's a rich, popular jock; and Nathaniel's a genius. Then . . . me."

"Technically, I'm not . . . ," I start to say, but Cooper drowns me out.

"Aww...poor Logan," he says. "Such low self-esteem. Should we have a pity party? Ooh, that could be our band name: Pity Party for Zero."

"Shut up, Cooper!" Jessa says, glaring at him.

"Did you know," I say loudly, "that zero is the most sophisticated number? It acts as a placeholder, holding all numbers together properly.

"Plus, zero is the hero of the number tree." (That line, from a children's book I used to love, just popped out.)

"Well," Jessa says, "Logan, you definitely hold our band together by keeping the beat. And it's better to be nice like you are than to be a popular jerk . . . I mean jock."

"I resemble that remark," Cooper says. He yawns. "Finley, buck up. You know we appreciate you. Have a Spree." He tosses Logan a candy. It bounces off a cymbal and hits the floor. Logan Finley's face turns as red as his hair.

Cooper walks over to Logan and hands him the whole roll of Sprees.

"Sprees for peace," Cooper says.

"And I believe we have a name for our band," Jessa announces. "It's quirky, like us. Ladies and gentlemen . . . Sprees for Peace!"

We all laugh. Then we vote. It's unanimous. We are Sprees for Peace.

Jessa has a great laugh. I look at her out of the corner of my eye and sigh quietly. I feel a light tap on my shoulder. I jump and spin around.

"Nathaniel man." It's Logan. "Have a Spree."

I take one and pop it into my mouth.

"Thanks," I say. When I turn back around, Jessa is gone.

CHAPTER FIVE
ARCHIMEDES IN MY BRAIN

I'm alone in my bedroom, laptop on my bed. I'm checking my e-mail. One from Wen, who has successfully received my sustainability essay. One cannot count on e-mail getting through due to China's Golden Shield firewalls. Wen says my ideas are interesting, and she'll write a longer e-mail later.

I'm deleting spam when my mother knocks on the door. I say to come in, and she does, with her phone in hand. My mother talks on the phone a lot, with her friends and her editors and her mother: my grandma. Grandma and I prefer to e-mail. I'm not too good on the phone. It's unpredictable what will come out of my mouth.

"Nathaniel, phone for you," my mother says, holding out the phone.

"I've been talking to Sharon," my mother says. Sharon has been her friend since September 19, 1996, when they met at a baby playgroup. I was my mother's baby. Sharon's daughter, Jessa—(yes, *that* same Jessa who is now in the band)—was the first baby to crawl over to me, and she took my shaky rattle. My mother says I handled it well. I don't recall this, as my memory files begin on December 25, 1997.

"Sharon says Jessa wants to speak with you." My mother gives me the phone. Suddenly, my hands feel sweaty and the phone slips out of my hand and hits the floor.

I dropped Jessa. Dumb klutz.

I pick up the phone.

"Hello?" I say.

"Hi, Nathaniel." Jessa's voice travels to my ear.

"Uh, what can I do for you?" I ask. I *hatehatehate* talking on the phone. It's totally awkward. I don't know how (or why) my mom does it so often.

"I was thinking about our set list," Jessa says. "Our four songs look good, don't you think?"

"Sure," I agree. I lay back on my bed. Glow-in-the-dark constellations are on my ceiling; but since it's not dark in here, they just look yellow. *No glow no glow no glow* ... Oops. Pay attention.

"We've got one girl power, one sentimental, one

boy pop, and, well, Cooper's wacky mix."

Open File: C:\My Files\band\songs\Cooper.avi (Date: 7/22/09)

"We need another song," Jessa says. "My sister's friends are picky, so we need one that's cool and fun."

"I've got it," Cooper says, positioning his electric guitar. He starts strumming and singing. (His voice isn't too good, so usually Logan and I are backup vocals.)

"I love you, you love me, we're a . . ."

"What?"

"Cooper!"

Even I know that the purple dinosaur song isn't exactly appropriate for teenagers.

"Wait," Cooper says. Suddenly, he's singing the words loud and fast and rocking out on his guitar.

"It's punk preschool!" Jessa laughs.

"Head, shoulders, knees, and toes!" I yell out. That was my favorite from preschool physical therapy, and the only "dance" I will do in public.

Cooper goes smoothly into a hard rock version of the song, and we all start banging our heads (and shoulders and knees, etc.).

Cooper's mix? Add it to our set list.

Close File.

"Yeah, those four are good," I say to Jessa.

"I still can't get the picture of Jade and her friends

in their glam outfits singing along to kiddie songs out of my head." Jessa giggles.

"Me either." Of course that's true, due to my lack of delete options in my memory.

"It should've been 'Head, shoulders, knees, and *stilet*toes,'" Jessa says, cracking herself up. "So, seriously, about our upcoming gig. My uncle says we'll be onstage for thirty minutes, and our set list only goes for twenty-two. Therefore, we need another song. I'm thinking it's time we did an original."

"An original," I echo. Echolalia is an autistic trait I have. Sometimes I automatically repeat the last part of what someone says. It's supposed to be a negative trait, but I find it comes in handy when I don't know what to say. Since Asperger's is on the high end of the autistic spectrum, I have some autistic traits mixed in with my profound intelligence traits. It's a confusing combination.

"Yes, our own song," Jessa says. "We need lyrics and music. Obviously, Logan is out since words are not his greatest talent. And Cooper would probably come up with something inappropriate. So that leaves you and me."

You and me? At least this echo stays in my head.

"Nathaniel?"

"I'm here," I say. "Okay, what can I do for you?"

"It's more like *with* me," Jessa says. "I think we should collaborate. Between the two of us, I think we can come up with something good. Unique."

"That sounds fine," I manage to say. *She wants to team up with me! Woohoo!*

"So my mom talked to your mom, and they said it's okay if you come over Monday after school—after *my* school," says Jessa. "If that works for you."

"Okay," I tell her. *Jessa invited me to her house!* It would be the first time I'd been over there since I (reluctantly) stopped trick-or-treating three Halloweens ago.

"Hold on," Jessa tells me. I hold on to the phone. "I've gotta go help my dad with his computer. Can I text or e-mail you about getting together Monday?"

"Yes," I say, and give her my e-mail address. I do not text. I am no good at spontaneous communication or condensed conversation.

"'Bye, Nathaniel, see you Monday," Jessa says.

"See you Monday," I say, and press off.

For the next hour I am unfocused. I try to read or solve math theorems, but I end up pacing back and forth in my room.

Back *Jessa invited me to her house.*

Forth *Jessa is pretty and smart.*

Back *Jessa, Jessa, Jessa ...*

Suddenly I stop pacing. I have a new thought. *Is this a date?* Jessa asked me to do something with her— *just the two of us.*

The thought of dating and Jessa becoming my girl-friend makes me start pacing again.

Boy. Girl. Boy. Girl. Back. Forth.

Wait! I stop.

Molly and I do activities together, just the two of us. Am I already dating Molly, and I just don't know it? Molly and I have never actually *talked* about our relationship. *I* think we're friends. Does Molly think something different?

I feel as if my brain is being squeezed. The pressure of figuring out girls weighs down my rational thoughts and out spills confusion.

$B = W_f$, where B is the buoyant force and W_f is the weight of fluid displaced. Archimedes' principle of Buoyancy.

I start pacing, faster this time, to run out my energy. Back. Forth. Back. Forth . . .

CHAPTER SIX

ACTION, REACTION, INERTIA, AND JOSHUA

"**B**ack! Come on, this way!" Molly is yelling and waving her hands at her bowling ball. It knocks down one pin.

"The ball can't hear you," I inform Molly, but as usual she does not listen to me. She throws her second ball down the lane and yells at it.

Whump. Whump. Whump. Three more pins go down slowly. Molly has arm strength issues, but it does not dampen her enthusiasm.

"Four!" she cheers. "One, two, three, four—add that to my score!"

The automatic scorekeeper updates her score to 72. That was her tenth frame.

"Molly, I ..." I've been trying to get this sentence out

since we were picking out our bowling balls. *I think you are a great friend. Is that how you think of me?* That was the statement I'd spent an hour last night preparing. But every time I've gotten up my nerve to try to clarify our relationship, something interrupts me.

"Your turn!" Molly interrupts me.

Sigh.

I go up, position my ball, take a few steps forward, and let go. *Rollrollroll* . . . strike! Oh yeah! I love to watch Newton's Laws of Motion in action. And reaction.

"That was sweet!" I hear an unfamiliar girl's voice yell.

"You rock, hottie!" another voice calls out.

I turn around and look at Molly. She is sitting at our scoring table drinking bottled lemonade from the vending machine.

I look beyond her. Up on the floor level, above the lanes, two girls—one blonde, one redhead—are waving to me.

"My friend thinks you're cute!" one of the girls yells, pointing first to her friend, then to me. The friend suddenly turns and runs off. The remaining girl shrugs and follows her friend.

I haven't said a word. Neither has Molly.

If I had said "hi" or "thank you," would they have laughed? Were those girls playing a joke on me? If they *were* serious and I'd responded to them, then I would have been answering to "hottie." Therefore, the probability of embarrassment would have been 100 percent. The only escape was silence. Which, when it comes to girls, I do well.

I'm a bit rattled, so I end up rolling a four and a two to close out the tenth frame.

"You beat me by sixty-two points," Molly says. "That's closer than last week!"

"Three points closer," I agree.

"Did you know that the book *Seabiscuit* is three hundred and thirty-nine pages long? And the movie is one hundred and forty-one minutes long?" Molly says, slipping off her bowling shoes. She, being an artist, has better fine motor skills than I do.

I stick my left foot out for her to undo the double knot she'd tied for me earlier.

"Did you know that technically I am not a genius?" I ask.

"Oh," Molly says. "But you got four strikes! That's good." She's untangled the laces on both of my shoes, and I take them off. We carry the shoes up to the bowling shoe person and trade them for our own. I wear mocs with no laces. Molly has leather riding boots. She wears them everywhere, including to her riding lessons, so don't ask how they smell.

Sensory override. I ignore the stench of manure and smile at Molly.

"I get to see my favorite Shetland, Theo, at the stables today." Molly jumps up and down, her brown curls bouncing, her fingers wiggling. I used to do that too: flap my hands and jump when I got excited. It felt good to have my whole body participate in my joy.

I was trained not to do that, though. So I don't jump or flap anymore. My mother says it's more okay for girls to be "bouncy," like cheerleaders. Which is illogical, because Molly would never be a cheerleader.

Except at a horse race.

"Hey, Sport." My father is here. I hadn't noticed him come in. He says hello to Molly and asks if I'm ready to go.

"I see my mom," Molly says. "'Bye, Nathaniel! 'Bye, Mr. Clark! Thank you for a nice time."

Molly still attends those social skills classes. Good manners are part of it.

"But . . . ," I say. I didn't get to say my statement.

"Good-bye, Molly," my father says. Molly walks away.

"Yeah, 'bye," I mumble.

"So, Nathaniel," my father says, "I saw those girls checking you out earlier." We walk through the automatic doors, out into the parking lot. It is autumn, but warm enough that my mother told me I did not need a jacket.

"Yeah," I say. Awkward.

"You should've talked to them," my father continues, "asked for their digits. Or are you and Molly now an item?"

Item? Digits?

I am completely lost in this line of questioning.

"Er," I stammer. Fortunately, I am saved from discussing this further by my poor proprioceptivity—sense of self in space—as I miss the curb, lurch out into the lot, and stumble into the side of a car. A slowly moving car backing out of its parking space.

"Sorry!" I call to the driver whose car I bumped.

"Your car is okay!" my father adds. He does not ask if I am okay.

I am okay.

My father beeps open his Lexus, and we both slide into opposite sides of the car. I am hoping someday he will hand me the keys and let me practice driving around the parking lot. I asked him on August 3 of this year and he said, "In a new Lexus? Are you stupid?"

At least I am not stupid enough to ask again today.

My father does not get me. I do not get my father. He calls himself a "people person." Right. People other than his own son.

When he lived with us, my father was a vice president at a public relations firm. My parents' divorce was finalized on August 12, 2005. My father bought a new house, started a new career, and married his new wife all in the next year. Not to mention the baby. Which I'd rather not.

Open File: C:\My Files\divorce\father.avi (Date: 8/15/05)

"Nathaniel, honey," my mother says as we are playing Triple Yahtzee. "You know that any time you miss or want to talk to your father, you can just call him."

"I won't," I say. "Four sixes in the 3x column, please."

My mom writes down 72—(24 x 3).

"I know your father has been . . . difficult." My mother rolls three ones, a five, and a two. "I wish he were kinder and more fun for you, but we've talked about this. It is not your fault."

"No, it's your fault because you married him," I say.

My mother laughs.

"You're right; you're right." She rolls out two dice. "Your dad seemed very charming when I met him. And, of course, it's because of him I have you."

"Is that good?" I ask, watching her final roll.

"What?" My mother looks at the dice. "Three ones—ugh. This Yahtzee roll? Not so good. You? Nathaniel Gideon Clark. Very, very good."

She leans over and kisses my head.

"I love you," she says. "To infinity."

"I love you infinity to the infinitieth power," I tell her. It's my turn to shake the cup. The dice fly out.

"Yahtzee!" I yell.

Close File.

I don't have to talk to my father during the 5.2 mile car ride. My father is on the phone with his personal assistant. They're on speaker, so I hear my father doing business.

"I'm sending you my latest work," he says. "Add it to the last chapter of *Passion into Action* and shoot it to my editor."

"Yes, sir," says the assistant. Then they discuss boring details, and I tune out.

My father is a well-known motivational speaker. He talks to audiences of hundreds of people. His personal assistant transcribes his speeches, which are turned into books, which become best-sellers.

Apparently there are many, many people who want to be motivated. It is baffling to me that my father is famous for telling people how to think and what to do.

We pull up to my father's house. There is a little boy riding a bicycle with training wheels in the driveway. The boy sees my father and jumps off the bike.

"Daddy!" he yells, racing toward the car. My

father parks and jumps out.

"Hey, Champ!" he says, catching the little guy in his arms and tossing him up onto his shoulders.

"Hi, 'Thaniel." He waves to me. I climb down from the Lexus.

"Hello, Joshua," I say. I grab my duffel bag and carry it toward the house. Behind me I hear Joshua's squeals of laughter as my father tickles him.

"Wanna do Westlemania!" Joshua shrieks.

"Sure, when we get inside," my father says. "The FatherNator has some new moves that'll turn you into jelly!"

More laughing.

Joshua Paul Clark is the son my father always wanted.

As I lug my duffel bag into the house, my father and Joshua are right behind me.

"I gonna be four!" Joshua announces.

"Yep," my father says. "So we're going to take the training wheels off. You're ready for a big-boy bike."

"Yayayayay!" Joshua runs off screaming. "Big-boy bike!"

Open File: C:\My Files\father\bike.avi (Date: 4/4/04)

"You can do it, Nathaniel, focus!" My father is teaching me to ride a two-wheeler. I do not want to ride a bicycle, but this is what

normal eight-year-olds do, says my father.

"I *am* focusing," I grumble. I really am trying. But what makes my father think I can do this when I can't even ride a bicycle with training wheels on? My feet do not respond to my brain's message to push the pedals in the right direction. And I have vestibular (balance) issues.

My center of gravity is a variable, not a constant.

Four years of occupational and physical therapy have proved that I should not be riding a bicycle. Hasn't my father read the evaluations?

"One more time!" he yells and pushes my back. "Pedal, pedal, pedal."

Obviously he has not.

The bike moves forward from the push, then it slows and tips over.

$$Acceleration = \frac{final\ velocity - initial\ velocity}{time}$$

$$a = \frac{0\ meter/second - 1\ meter/second}{2\ seconds}$$

$$a = -0.5\ meter/second^2$$

(or $0.5\ meter/second^2$ backward)

"Remind me," I say from the ground. The bicycle is on top of me, and my helmet has slipped over my eyes. "Exactly what is my motivation?"

"Your motivation is to have fun!" My father's voice is louder and tight. "Kids ride bikes! Bikes are fun!"

As my father "motivates" me, I lie back and close my eyes.

"Did you know," I say, "that four cubed is sixty-four and sixty-four cubed is 262,144?"

"What?" My father's pulling the bike off me.

"Today's date," I remind him. "April 4, '04. 4-4-4. And 444 times two equals 888, which is my age in each units place!"

I have some more fun with mental math calculations,while my father uses words rated PG-13 and R.

Close File.

CHAPTER SEVEN
POP GOES THE GENIUS BALLOON

"Please pass the potatoes," my father says. Looking at us, we would seem like a typical family eating dinner together. Of course we're *not* typical—especially me—and this isn't my family. It is my father's.

"Nathaniel," my father's new wife says. "How are things going?"

Her name is Rachel. She is very different from my father's first wife, my mother. My mother has light brown hair. Rachel's is dark brown, almost black, and curly. My mother's hair is straight. My mother has blue eyes. Rachel's are brown.

Rachel works at an accounting firm. Joshua is in daycare from 7:30 a.m. until 6:00 p.m. five days a week. My mother works from home and has never put me in daycare. Or school. (Except for one year of preschool, which was okay, although I told my mother I "don't fit in with my peers.")

I love my mother. I don't love Rachel. But she's pretty nice—a lot nicer than my father. So I tolerate her questions even though I would rather be left alone.

"Everything is fine." I give my standard answer. But then I surprise myself. I keep talking.

"Except for one problem I have. I can't figure out how to solve it."

"That must be frustrating for you," Rachel says. She leans over and wipes something off Joshua's face.

"It is." I eat my crescent roll. I'm a carbohydrates addict. I ignore the meat on my plate. Gag.

"You're experiencing a life blockage?" My father looks up from his plate. *Oh, great. He's using his motivational-speaker speak. Why did I say anything?*

"Mmmh," I mumble.

"De-ssert, de-ssert," Joshua starts chanting.

"Finish your peas first," my father says. Then he turns back to me.

"When one encounters a life blockage, it can be useful to form a support group to facilitate its dissolution."

"English translation, Steven?" Rachel says.

"Nathaniel could get a group of people together for a problem-solving session," my father clarifies. "Hey, supply some drinks and munchies, and you could turn it into a party!"

"My problem is not frivolous!" I'm horrified. I have an image of GENIUS balloons and a GENIUS cake.

"I having a party," Joshua announces. "It's monster trucks, and I get a monster truck cake—*vrrrrooom, rmmm*!"

"That's right, sweetie." Rachel smiles at her son. Joshua looks just like her. Except that he's a boy. Same dark, curly hair and brown eyes.

He looks nothing like my father. But I do. It is ironic that the son who looks like him acts completely different from him, and the son who looks nothing like him is a gregarious, sports- and truck-loving Daddy's boy. It works for me. I'd choose his appearance genes over his personality genes any day.

Did I mention that my father, with his blond hair, blue eyes, and (spray-on) tan is considered good-looking? When he was twenty-five, he was named one of Boston's "Most Eligible Bachelors" in a magazine. That was before he married my mother. I find it embarrassing when people comment on how alike we look. I do *not* have a spray-on tan. Sheesh.

"Okay." My father is still talking. "It could be more like a think tank, where you and your friends put your heads together to come up with a solution."

"I don't want people touching my head," I say,

envisioning a creature with fused heads and multiple limbs. "I can't think when people are touching me."

"It's a figure of speech, Nathaniel," Rachel says. "Putting your heads together means everyone is thinking about the same problem at the same time."

Oh. I despise idioms. Why can't people just say things straightforward?

"De-ssert! De-ssert!" Joshua chants.

"Inside voice, Joshie," Rachel says. "I'll go get dessert if you say 'please.'"

"Please," Joshua and my father both say, making Joshua laugh. My father reaches over and rubs his hand in Joshua's hair. He never did that to me when I was little. I probably would have bitten his hand. Not on purpose, just that I've never liked my head touched.

Rachel comes back with a plate of brownies, and soon we are all busy chewing. Thankfully, my Problem has been forgotten. By everyone except me. I let the taste of chocolate drown out my negative thoughts. Chocolate = Mmmm!

Later that evening . . .

Wikipedia. "The Amazing Race 7."

I'm scrolling down the Wiki, reading about my favorite TV show. I absolutely love *The Amazing Race.* They call it a "reality" show, but in reality very few people get to travel around the globe and do exciting challenges in the quest to win one million dollars. I have memorized all the teams from previous seasons, the place they finished, and why they were eliminated. I have every season's travel destinations and competition challenges filed away. (My favorites? Location: Mendoza, Argentina, or Almaty, Kazakhstan. Challenge: "Pony Up or Tee It Up" Detour in Montego Bay, Jamaica.)

I plan to get on the show when I hit the eligibility requirement of age twenty-one. All my knowledge will make me a top contender for the million dollars. Of course, I'll need a competent partner, because you compete in pairs. I've already asked my grandmother, who says she'll do it if her knees have been replaced by then.

Even though I've seen this information many times, I still enjoy looking over the statistics and graphs and contestant elimination patterns. In Aspergerese, my hobby is called a "special interest" or "perseveration." My father calls it an "obsessive waste of time." I'm sorry, Dad, but you've *been* (pronounced with the British long ē) eliminated from *my* personal reality show, so your opinion does not count.

I scroll. Ooh . . . this is when the final two teams battle: good versus evil. At the last minute the good team overtakes the manipulative evil team to take home one million doll—

"Ahhhhh!" I scream. I'm being attacked!

"Westlemania!" is the last thing I hear before sensory overload gushes through my system. I jump out of my swivel chair, adrenaline exploding. Unfortunately, my "flight" reaction results in my attacker's "flight" across the room.

Thud!

Joshua hits the wall and lands on the floor. He is wearing a diaper-that-looks-like-underwear and a black cape. I watch as his mouth opens and emits a piercing wail.

Rachel and my father come running into my room.

"Joshie!" Rachel scoops up her sobbing son.

"What happened?" my father demands.

I know I am supposed to say something or do something, but my systems shut down. All that's left is my instinct to flee.

I race out of the room, experiencing Bernoulli's principle in action. As I approach Joshua, his wails grow louder. Then as I run past him out my bedroom door, his sound gets quieter. By the time I reach the laundry room down the hallway, the noise is almost bearable. I go into the laundry room and shut the door. Silence. Darkness. Relief. I sit down on the floor, leaning my body against the washing machine. Its surface is cool against my back, and I close my eyes, hoping everything around me will cool down, too.

The door opens. No such luck. Light pours in, and I look up to face the consequences. To my surprise, I see Joshua.

"Hide and seek!" he whispers. "I found you!"

He closes the door behind him, and the room goes dark again.

"We hide together," Joshua says. I feel him sit down by my side, his breath against my neck. He smells like apples.

"I didn't mean to hurt you," I say. Finally, my brain and mouth are cooperating with an appropriate thing to say. "I got surprised, that's all."

"You fweaked out." Joshua giggles.

"Yeah," I agree.

We sit there quietly in the dark. I hear my father and Rachel calling our names. Their voices get closer, louder. It sounds as if they are standing in the hallway just outside the laundry room. I have an idea.

"Let's jump out and surprise *them*," I say.

"One, two, fwee . . . boo?" Joshua asks.

"One, two, three, boo," I say. "Let's do it."

So together we count to three and jump out of the laundry room, yelling, "Boo!"

"Aack!" Rachel jumps back.

"What the—," my father growls.

"We got you! We got you!" Joshua hops up and

down in his underwear, cape flapping.

My father leans down and swings Joshua up into his arms. He looks at me. He starts to yell at me.

"Steven!" Rachel says. "Stop it. You'll upset the boys." Surprisingly, my father shuts up.

"I told Joshua it was an accident," I say. "I'm sorry."

"Well, Joshua seems fine," Rachel says gently. "But my heart is still pounding from you two jumping out! Silly boys."

"We silly boys!" Joshua agrees. "Wight, 'Thaniel?"

"Um, right," I say. *Me silly. O-kay.*

"Time for bed, Big Guy," my father tells Joshua. He carries his son down the hallway toward Joshua's room, Rachel trailing close behind.

"Night, 'Thaniel!" Joshua calls.

"Good night, Joshua," I reply dutifully. My mind is already on my obsession. I head back to my room to watch season seven's final episode of *The Amazing Race* on YouTube. Although I've watched it at least ten times, I still feel a thrill when the team I favor ekes it out to win the million dollars.

CHAPTER EIGHT
GENIUS VERSUS LIFE

Bzzt.

It's Monday, 3:00 p.m. EST.

Bzzt. I press the buzzer once more and wait.

The door opens. There stands Jessa. I have the sudden urge to say "Trick or Treat," which is what I'd said the last time I was here. But that would be weird. Today is not Halloween.

"Is this a date?" I blurt out.

Great, that was even weirder. I feel like an asp-hole.

"Hi, Nathaniel," Jessa says. "Come on in."

I walk into her house. It smells like cinnamon.

"Let's go into the kitchen," Jessa says. "I made cinnamon rolls—not from scratch or anything—they came in one of those tubes that pop when you open them. We can work on our song in there."

I follow Jessa. Her shiny dark hair bounces a little as she walks. She sits down at a table with a pan of frosted cinnamon rolls and two plates. I sit down where a plate is.

Now what?

"Want one?" Jessa asks, tearing a roll out of the pan. White frosting oozes down the sides. I have to look away. I can practically feel the sticky pastiness between my fingers.

"Uh, no thank you," I say, wiping my hands on my jeans. Sensory issues had kept me from ooey things such as Play-Doh, finger paints, and pudding my whole life. Gooey = gag.

"Nathaniel!" Jessa's mother, Sharon, pops into the room. "You're so huge! You look great! I've missed you!"

A feeling of comfort settles over me. My mother's friend Sharon has always accepted me, been nice to me, since I was little.

I let her give me a little squeeze around my neck.

"I'll let you two get to work," Sharon says. "Don't be a stranger, Nathaniel."

"I can't be a stranger," I remind her. "I've known you since toddlerhood."

"Very true!" Jessa's mom grins and grabs a cinnamon roll. The icing stretches and drips.

I look away.

"Nice to see you, Miss Sharon," I say. I hope my good manners aren't negated by lack of eye contact.

"I'll be in my office if you need me," Jessa's mother says. "And Jessa, don't forget rule number sixteen."

"Mom." Jessa groans. "You can leave now. Love you, 'bye."

When Miss Sharon is gone, I ask, "What's rule number sixteen?"

"Oh, my parents gave me a list of eighteen rules I have to follow until I'm eighteen and out of the house," Jessa says, swallowing a bite. "Rule number sixteen is no dating until I'm sixteen."

"Oh," I respond brilliantly.

"So, to answer your question from before? No, this isn't a date," Jessa says, and finishes her roll.

"Uh, yeah, no, of course I didn't think it was. I just, umm . . . ," I stammer.

"Not that I wouldn't be lucky to date a guy like you," Jessa says, picking up the tray of rolls and putting them in the refrigerator. "Want a vitamin water?"

"Yes," my mouth speaks. *Huh???* my mind thinks.

Jessa comes back to the table with two clear bottles of vitamin water, a pen, and a pad of paper.

"Did you know," I say, "that you can demonstrate Snell's Law with these objects?"

Jessa takes a sip of water and looks at me.

I take the pen and paper and write on it, then push the paper over for her to read.

$$n_1 \sin (\theta_1) = n_2 \sin (\theta_2)$$

"See?" I uncap my vitamin water and drink. "That's Snell's Law." I take another gulp and . . . miss my mouth.

"Looks more like Spill's Law," says Jessa. "Joke, Nathaniel. It's no big deal."

I am splattered but not soaked.

"Spill's Law," I manage. "I get it." Geekloserklutz-dorkidiot.

"Hey!" Jessa says. "Remember the time we were like five and my sister Jade was seven, and we were all eating popsicles and . . ."

Open File: C:\My Files\Jessa\popsicles.avi (Date: 8/18/01)

"Aaaaah! My popsicle broke off!" Jade screams.

I put my hands over my ears and look at her. All I see is Jade holding an empty stick. We are out in their backyard: Jessa, Jade, and me. Our mothers are in the girls' house doing Grown-up Talk, which I think should include me since I have the vocabulary of an adult; but when I tell my mother, she says I'm missing the point.

"Where'd it go?" Jessa asks.

"Down my shirt!" Jade wails, and jumps up and down. Little chunks of colored ice rain down on the ground around her bare feet.

"A freezing rain advisory has been issued for Jade City," I announce. (I am in my weather-alert-obsession phase.)

I look at Jessa. She catches my eye. And for whatever reason, we both start laughing so hard, even Jade finally joins in.
Close File.

"I remember," I tell Jessa.

"What I remember most is that you looked me right in the eyes," Jessa says. "Usually you'd look off in some other direction when you were talking, and my mom said that was because you had Asperger's syndrome. She said it was hard for you to do certain things, and Jade and I were like 'Yeah, right.' We thought everything was easy for you because you were so smart."

"Wow," I say. They talked about me? Weird.

"I think your mom and my mom were just making sure Jade and I understood that it was okay that you were different." Jessa finishes her water and smiles. "But you know what? To us you were just Nathaniel. Looking back, I don't know how you put up with me and Jade. We were annoying!"

"No, you were fun," I say, looking at the table. I never really needed friends like most kids did, but I guess I was lucky that I had some anyway.

"So," I repeat in delayed echolalia, "I couldn't look you in the eyes, and you thought things were easy for me because of my intellect?"

"Yeah ... wait!" Jessa grabs the pen and starts writing

on a piece of paper.

"Wait?" I echo.

"Shhh!" Jessa shushes me. Then she turns the paper around and pushes it toward me.

"I can read upside down," I inform her. "It doesn't take a genius to rotate text mentally."

"Just read it," Jessa says. "Out loud, so I can hear it, please."

So I read:

You can't look me in the eyes,
And I can't see past your brain.
Our vision is clouded,
And it's hard to explain

"It's not that hard to explain," I say. "According to diagnostic criteria, Asperger's is defined as—"

"No, no, Nathaniel," Jessa interrupts. "It's the beginning of our song! Think in lyrics—not logic."

"That's easy for you," I complain. "You're neurotypical. Normal. I'm just an Aspie geek, with asynchronal talents."

"What?" Jessa asks. She grabs the paper and starts scribbling again.

"'Asynchrony,'" I say, getting a little annoyed. "It means I'm profoundly gifted at some things and a total loser at other things. . . . What are you writing?"

"Sorry," Jessa mumbles, "this is good stuff." She writes and writes. Finally she puts down the pen. Then she starts singing what she wrote in a soft, melodious tune I don't recognize.

You can't look me in the eyes,
And I can't see past your brain.
Our vision is clouded,
And how do you explain
That you're more than just a test score
Or an off-the-charts IQ?
Geek! Nerd! Loser!
Is what you see.
And you're thinking, "I'm just me. . . ."
Neurotypical—what's that?
And asynchrony?
Neuro-what?
Async-huh?
You're a teenage mystery.
Conflicts: person versus person, and
Person versus self.
It's man versus nature . . .

She stops and looks at me.

"And society itself," I say, getting into the whole

song-rhyming thing. Jessa writes down my three words.
And taps her pen against her bottom lip.

"It's genius versus life," she says suddenly, and begins writing again quickly. "You're a genius versus life.
You're fighting for your life."

"Overly dramatic and inaccurate," I critique her. "I
am not officially a genius, and I'm not in a fight for my
existence. And you've misspelled asynchrony." I add an
h to the word, using Jessa's pen.

"So it's easy being you?" Jessa asks.

"No!" I surprise myself with my forceful response.
"It's hard to be outside of my own world. It's hard to
deal with people—normal people, not like me."

Once again, Jessa's writing furiously.

"Here," she says after a few minutes. "Read this."

But it's hard to go outside,
So much easier to hide
From all the people,
Normal people
Not like me.
Who can't see. Who can't see me.
We're all mindblind.

"Mindblind," I say. "It's an Aspie term, meaning
'I can't seem to guess what other people are thinking.'

I am clueless about any perspective but mine."

"Yeah, I read a good book by a person with Asperger's," Jessa tells me. "That's where I got the word mindblind. But I think it applies to a lot of us who don't have AS, too. Don't you?"

"I don't know." I shrug. "I'm too mindblinded to figure it out."

"Well, I feel brain-dead after all that work," Jessa says. "But I think that with a few tweaks, the song will be really good. Kinda indie, kinda obscure, totally relevant. What do you think?"

"Um," I say. "It's a little personal."

"That's what songwriters do." Jessa grins. "They write about what they know and pour their heart out on the page."

"Yeccch." I visualize a human heart spilling out of a person's chest cavity onto a piece of paper.

Jessa's mom walks back into the room.

"Nathaniel, your mom's here," she informs me. "She's waiting in the car out front. Before you leave, how'd it go?"

"Human organs were splattered during the making of this song," I say, still not over the heart visual. "But it is good. Jessa is really good at writing songs."

Jessa's face turns pink. I'm not sure if that's good or bad.

"Thanks." She smiles. (Whew.) "We make a great team. Plus, this is my passion. That's what I want to do when I'm older—have a career as a singer-songwriter." Jessa pauses. "And be an opthalmologist," she adds. "I've always been fascinated with eyes."

"My daughter, the singing eye doctor." Miss Sharon shakes her head.

"I think it's unique," I say. "I will be your first patient."

"Only if you look me in the eyes." Jessa laughs.

"It's against everything I stand for," I say. "But I'll do it so that my vision isn't cloudy from things I can't explain. . . ."

I leave Jessa's house with us both laughing really hard and Miss Sharon saying, "You two are crazy."

That was the best time ever.

Jessa = LOVE

My mind might be blind, but my heart works just fine.

Mindblind

By Jessa Rose and Nathaniel Clark

(Jessa) solo

You can't look me in the eyes,
And I can't see past your brain.
Our vision is clouded,
And how do you explain

That you're more than just a test score
Or an off-the-charts IQ?
Geek! Nerd! Loser!
Is what they see.
And you're thinking, "I'm just me. . . ."

(All rap-style)
Neurotypical—what's that?
And *asynchrony*?
Neuro—what?
Async—huh?
You're a teenage mystery.
(Jessa) solo
Conflicts: person versus person, and
Person versus self.
It's man versus nature and society itself.
It's genius versus life.
You're a genius versus life.
You're fighting for your life.
And how do you explain
Who you are? It's so hard.
Weirdo—genius—loner is what they see
And you are thinking,
"I'm just me."
But it's hard to go outside
So much easier to hide

From all the people,
Normal people
Not like you.
(Nathaniel—solo?) tempo slows
Not like me.
Who can't see. Who can't see me.
We're all mindblind.
(All rap-style/rock out)
Mindblind—what is *that*?
Mindless—*what*?
Blindness—*huh*?
Just be "you," just be "me,"
Just break free.
(Jessa solo) tempo slow—no instrumental
Just break free.
Open your eyes . . .
And see.

CHAPTER NINE
NO CLUE

I spend the next few days trying to distract myself from thinking about that song. I do not want to disappoint Jessa, but I am an extremely private person. Objectively, it is a very good song. But do I really want to sing it?

I can't stop thinking about it. I need to stop perseverating and turn my brain in a different direction.

I get on my computer and start a new project. It is a fantasy—*Amazing Race*—with individuals competing through a time portal.

I have been waiting and waiting to reach the age of twenty-one to be eligible to go on the reality show. I plan to be the first genius with Asperger's syndrome to win *The Amazing Race*. (By then I *will* be an official genius. I will.)

In season fifteen (2009), the unthinkable almost

happened. Someone almost beat me to it. A guy named Zev, who has Asperger's and is profoundly gifted, was on the show. But he did not win, so my dream remains intact.

Back to my fantasy reality show. I've decided to use competitors who have Asperger's, or, in the case of historical figures, have been speculated to have had it.

I'm working on it when my mom taps on the door and pokes her head in the room.

"Nathaniel, when did you eat last?" she asks.

"I don't know," I respond, typing away.

"Nathaniel," Mom repeats, "are you hungry?"

I stop typing and think about it. My stomach does feel empty.

"Yes," I tell her. "But I'm working on something."

"I hope it has to do with your graduate school applications," my mother says.

Uh. Just because I'm taking an academic break doesn't mean it will last forever. Next fall I will be enrolled in graduate school. My problem? I don't know which school, and I don't know which degree program. There are many careers I could pursue. It's all too overwhelming. I can't figure out how to begin.

"I think I'll make a sandwich." I save my file and log off the computer.

"You're avoiding my question." My mother sighs.

"No, I'm not." I grin at her. "You asked if I was hungry, and my answer is 'Yes, I am.'"

"Good save," she says. As I pass her, she pulls me into a hug. I make my arms wrap around her and squeeze back.

Then I look down at the top of my mother's head. I am still not used to being taller than she is. Six and three-tenths inches taller to be exact. I've spent most of my life looking up to her; watching her for cues on how to act. I notice a feeling inside that is not hunger.

"I love you, Mom," I say.

"I love you too, sweetie," Mom says. "You're my favorite person in the whole universe."

She's been saying that since I was little.

Maybe that's why she and my father got divorced. He's the type who always has to be number one.

Plus, he's a jerk.

In the kitchen, I work on my sandwich. Spreading peanut butter on bread is not so easy for me. I tend to dig up too much p.b. and smush the bread or scoop too little and tear the bread. I concentrate on making a decent sandwich. When I am finished, I carefully pour water into a glass and join my mother at the table. She's drinking from a mug full of green tea. I force myself to ignore the grassy smell and start eating.

"Nathaniel," my mother says. Sip. "You've been

procrastinating about filling out your applications. Can you tell me why?"

I look down. Chew. Chew.

"You do remember," my mother continues, "that grad school is *your* idea. When your gap year ends this spring, you have many other options. You don't have to be so *driven*, like you were when you were getting your college degree."

"Did you know that a jet-powered Rolls Royce called Thrust SSC can be *driven* up to speeds of 763 mph?" I say.

"Did *you* know that MIT and Harvard have deadlines coming up soon?" my mother says. Fortunately, we live less than an hour from Boston, so I can live at home and commute to classes. Next year my parents would have to drive me, but the year after I could drive myself. If I have my own car.

"A Rolls Royce would be an ideal sixteenth birthday gift for me," I muse. "Or a Ferrari."

"Sure, no problem," my mother says. "First you have to get your learner's permit, pass your driving exam, and earn at least a million dollars."

"I do have a lot to get working on, don't I?" I swallow my last bit of sandwich and wash it down with my drink. "Graduate school, make a million dollars, become an official genius . . ."

My mother gets up from the table and dumps the remaining contents of her mug into the sink.

"Are you still stuck on that genius thing?" she asks. "Nathaniel . . . I thought that ridiculous obsession was gone. You haven't mentioned it in a long time."

"It's not a ridiculous obsession," I mutter. I can feel frustration in my body. *Not a genius, not a genius, not a . . .*

The thing with having Asperger's is that my mood can go from fine to not fine in seconds. It's black or white. Calm or meltdown.

I stomp over to the counter and slam down my plate and glass. I suppose I'm lucky they don't break, but I don't feel the luck. Instead I feel angry.

"This place smells disgusting!" I notice the gross tea leaves stuck to the edge of the sink and want to gag. *Not a genius, not a genius . . .*

"Nathaniel," my mother says, "take some deep breaths."

Her calm voice annoys me even more.

"Don't patronize me!" I shout. "I'm not stupid, stupid!"

Pause.

Oops.

Forty-five minutes later.

I'm scrubbing the bathtub.

After my meltdown I was sent to my room (no electronics allowed), where I did some minor damage to my closet door after throwing my Rubik's Cube at it. The Rubik's Cube sustained major damage. As I was crawling around the floor picking up colored puzzle guts, my rage disappeared. Just like that. It comes fast and leaves fast.

And often leaves me feeling, well, stupid.

So I went and apologized to my mother. She understands my meltdowns, but she doesn't let me get away with them.

Hence the bathtub. Sponge. All-natural cleaning spray. My consequences usually involve cleaning. I suspect my mother is secretly pleased when she has to punish me, because it gets her out of doing housework. But I could be wrong. I'm often incorrect in my assumptions about other people's feelings and intentions.

"Mom?" I call out. She pops her head into the bathroom.

"Yes?" she says.

"Do you secretly enjoy having to give me consequences because it reduces your housecleaning?"

"Yes," my mother says. "I enjoy every minute of your temper tantrums and hope for them every day so my bathroom gets cleaned."

I think for a moment.

"Are you being serious or sarcastic?" I ask.

"Ninety percent sarcastic, ten percent serious," she responds.

I scrub some more. The porcelain is brighter. I am almost done.

"Sweetie?" my mom says, leaning against the doorway. I look at her—really look at her instead of just glance. Her light brown hair is shorter than I remember, and she has on a blue shirt that says MATH OLYMPIAD 2009. *Hey, that is my shirt.* She looks young for a forty-year-old person. She also looks a little tired.

"Sweetie," my mom repeats.

"What?" I tune back into her words.

"Do you remember what you wanted to be when you grew up, back when you were little?"

Open File: C:\My Files\genius\career_first.avi (Date: 12/1/99)

"Juice boxes, $3.99. Four apples at .50¢ apiece, $2.00. Bread, $2.29." I'm reading along with the screen. I love it here in aisle seven. The beep of the barcode reader, the *wrsssh* of the checkout conveyor belt.

But then everything changes.

"Stop!" I yell. "Violation in aisle seven!"

My mother and the grocery clerk—"Martha! 6 years of Service Excellence!"—stop and stare at me.

"Pricing violation!" I inform them. "The bread is on sale this week for $2.09."

The clerk runs it through again, this time on the sale price tag. $2.09.

"Don't forget to delete the first bread," I remind her. As she fixes and completes our purchase, I turn to my mom and say, "You would think that after six years of service excellence, Martha would be more aware of pricing errors."

"Nathaniel, shhhh!" My mother's eyebrows turn into a V. "I'm sorry . . . Martha, is it? Thank you very much."

She steers our bag-filled cart away from the checkout counter. I've got the receipt in my hands, reading it as usual, when I hear behind me—from aisle seven—Excellent Martha's voice: "Brat."

Close File.

"I wanted to work at the supermarket and be a checkout person." I smile a bit at the thought.

"Well, you'll be fifteen in January," my mother says. "That's the age you need to be to work there."

"Work in a grocery store?" I say. "I can't do that! That wouldn't get me anywhere!"

"You have plenty of time to get 'somewhere,'" my mother says. "I think you'd really enjoy yourself."

I *would* enjoy myself. I would give Excellent Service and have control over the whole checkout process. But that's just a childish dream.

"I'm finished," I say, making one last swipe at the tub.

"Good work," my mother says.

And I'm free again to do my fantasy computer project, Amazing Race. I wish *I* could jump into a time portal and fast-forward to the place where I am a renowned and official genius.

I hope I don't have to go too far into the future. I wish I could invent a time portal.

I go into my room and close the door.

I'm settling into my ergonomic swivel chair when it swivels left. I can't help but see the graduate school apps. For a moment I indulge in fantasy.

I park my Ferrari in a space at MIT's student parking lot. I get out. Some students are staring at my car, others at me. "It's him," I hear some say. "The guy who ..."

The guy who what? Discovered/Invented/Created . . . what? New fantasy.

I park my Ferrari in a space at Harvard's student parking lot. I get out and confidently head to my next class. I've gotten all As so far, of course, and my professor has asked me to teach his class today since I'm such an expert in ... What?

What building would I be heading to? The computer science lab? The mathematics building? The one for international business (emphasis on Asia)?

The cafeteria where I wear an apron in school colors and work as a cashier?????

Ugh. I have no clue.

I swivel right and face my computer. I stare at my screensaver—a Rube Goldberg diagram—and wish I could just stay here for the rest of my life. What is that joke? "How do you get rid of Asperger's? Stay in a room alone." That's because an Aspie is only "different" when there is another human—or group of humans—to compare him to.

Okay, back to my imaginary *Amazing Race*. I've chosen the players, typed up their geographic destinations for each leg of the race. Now I get to decide the order in which they place. Who wins, who loses.

I decide to eliminate Newton first. He was a true genius in mathematics, physics, and astronomy; and he invented calculus. But—he was also anxious, obsessive, almost never laughed, and spent most of his time alone. Once he stuck a sewing needle into his eye socket just to see what would happen.

No, Sir Isaac Newton wouldn't be able to handle a TV reality show. Sorry, Sir Isaac, you have been eliminated.

I have lots of fun ranking everyone. When I'm done, I save my work and check my e-mail.

I delete spam and then open a message from Logan.

It's cc'd to Cooper and Jessa.

Hey. Have the flu. Can't make practice Fri. Sorry.

Next, I open a response from Jessa, cc'd to Logan and Cooper.

Logan, no worries! just feel better! N & C: practice canceled this week. we can just use the songs we've already got for the bat mitzvah. no time to rehearse any new ones. (N, hope that's ok w/you). J

"Yes!" I shout, leaning back in my chair. A whoosh of breath comes out of me. I did not realize just how worried I was about that mindblind song. No worries!

Theoretically, it would be fine to have a song inspired by me. But, in reality, I'd much rather have a law, such as Newton's three Laws of Motion, Faraday's law of induction, Bernoulli's principle (air pressure). Boyle, Ohm, Hubble all have laws. Nathaniel Gideon Clark's law of . . . something.

Well, I can't control whether I am a genius or not. But I *can* control my geniuses. I go back to my *Amazing Race* fantasy computer project.

It is so cool.

CHAPTER TEN
PANICPANICPANICPANIC

Saturday afternoon. Molly and I are bowling our second game. It is my turn to pick up the ball and bowl, but instead I say, "Molly? Is this a date?"

She looks blankly at me.

"Not like a date on a calendar; I know it's *that* kind of date." I'm babbling. "What I would like to know is if this is a boy-girl romantic date-type date?"

"I hope not . . . ," Molly says slowly, looking in the direction of the arcade in the distance.

I look down at my bowling shoes. They really are ugly.

"I hope not," Molly repeats (as if hearing it once wasn't enough for me), "because I don't think my boyfriend would like that very much."

"Your boyfriend?" I say. My head jerks up in surprise.

"Yes." Molly sighs. "Alex Josef. He works at the stable where I ride. Sometimes he takes a break, and we ride together. On the same horse!"

Molly starts giggling. This is the first time I've ever seen her happy about anything besides a horse or a decent (for her) round of bowling. Even I—misinterpreter of others' emotions—can tell she's really happy.

"That is great, Molly," I say. Mission accomplished. Back to bowling . . . although the rest of my game suffers after that due to Molly's inability to cease talking about her boyfriend.

"He knows as much about equine history as I do," Molly says. I bowl a split.

"And he looks *so* cute while he's grooming the horses, I just want to kiss him," Molly says. My next ball goes right down the middle, between the pins.

By the last frame I have given up.

"Sometimes, in the corner of the stable behind the bales of hay, we rub noses in affection, just like horses do." Molly jumps and flaps. "Alex calls it nuzzling."

I throw a gutter ball. What do neurotypicals say? TMI. Too much information.

"Okay, there's my father," I say, happy—perhaps for the first time ever—to see him.

"Okay," Molly says. "I hope your bowling improves next week!"

Only if you wear a horse muzzle, I think. That was not nice. I wave and smile and say "See you next week!" to Molly. Molly Muzzlemouth. That is pretty funny. I allow myself an internal *Ha!*

Then it's off with my father to his house. I'm hoping to make serious progress on my grad school applications, which are in the briefcase I am carrying. I lay the briefcase gently at my feet as I sit down in the passenger seat of the Lexus and press the recline button.

Aaah. Silence. Tune out the world.

"Hey, Bud, I've got some fun plans for you tonight," my father says. Uh-oh. My father and I have different definitions of FUN.

"One of my best clients has a son your age," my father says. "And he's having a party tonight."

"So what does that have to do with me?" I ask. Then it hits me. I can be so dumb.

"You're invited!" my father says. "My client and his, er, girlfriend will be chaperoning the party. Guys and girls your age, good food, music . . . good times. Makes me wish I were your age again."

"I can't go," I inform him. "I'm working on my graduate school applications this weekend."

"You can do that anytime." My father dismisses what I thought was a foolproof excuse. "You have hours, a day, every day, for (R-rated word)'s sake. No, tonight you are going to the party. I'll drop you off at nine o'clock."

I shut my eyes.

"One cubed is one, two cubed is eight, three cubed is twenty-seven, sixty-four, one twenty-five, two sixteen . . ."

"Stop that!" My father smacks his hand on the dashboard. "You're going and that's that!"

"Sixty-six miles per hour, one hundred and six point two hundred sixteen kilometers per hour, due southeast, twenty-one thousand miles on odometer, one hundred and four point five FM, one-third gas tank full, sixty-eight degrees Fahrenheit outside, twenty degrees Celsius, two hundred and ninety-three degrees Kelvin." I search the car's interior for any numbers I can find.

"You're going to the party, and you will not spout any of your nonsense; you will be a normal teenager, and you will have fun!" my father yells.

"I'm not going," I say.

"Then I will take away your computer and sell it," my father says, his quieter voice even scarier than his shouting. "And I will e-mail my buddy Pete, and tell him you've changed your mind and you would *love* to join intramural basketball. Pete says his team meets three nights a week, with one—sometimes two—games on the weekends."

I'm going to the party.

I do not say a word for the next five hours. It is not so difficult to do because Rachel and her son are visiting her parents, who live eighty-four miles away in Amherst. And it does not appear that my father has anything to say to me either. We both shut ourselves in our respective rooms. I throw my briefcase on the floor, not bothering to open it. I lay down on the bed.

Then I sleep.

"Nathaniel, time to get ready."

I hear my father knocking on my door. I ignore him. Maybe I can will my mind to send my body to a parallel universe where there is no party and where my father leaves me alone. I concentrate on vibrating my molecules to a place where there could be a deviation of the inverse square principle of Newton's Law of Universal Gravitation.

"Now, Nathaniel."

Darn molecules. Darn Newton's law.

"I'm coming," I say, rolling off the bed.

The bedroom door opens. My father does not look happy. Surprise, surprise. (Note: use of sarcasm instead of literal language. My father looking unhappily at me is not really a surprise.)

"You have ten minutes to fix your hair, get dressed, and grab something to eat," he says. "You can eat it in the car."

And he's gone.

I look in the full-length mirror. What does it mean "fix my hair"? It's not broken. My hair is my hair. After I comb it, it looks more blond, more straight lines. Does that mean it's fixed? Then I check out my clothes. Jeans. T-shirt. I *am* dressed.

I go down the long hallway, down the grand staircase, to the front door. I suppose some people would be impressed by this house. I am not one of them.

"No food?" My father frowns.

"Not hungry," I mumble.

"Hmmmm . . ." My father looks me over. Then he opens a closet door and pulls out something.

"Put this on." It's a brown leather jacket. I want to argue, but when I take it, I feel its texture. Nice. Very, very nice.

"You've got only one chance to make a first impression," my father says. "This jacket—which is mine, by the way, so be careful with it—says 'casual luxury.'"

I step over to the beveled front-hall mirror and wave my hand.

"Hi, I'm Casual Luxury," I say.

"Wiseass," says my father. But then he comes over and stands behind me. *Whoa*. Our reflections show how alike we look.

"I must be Casual Luxury, Senior," my father says.

"Or Senior Citizen Casual Luxury." The joke pops out of my mouth before I can stop it. I fully expect to be in trouble now.

Instead my father laughs.

"Don't count this old man out yet," he says. Then we go outside and get into the car. I have no idea what just happened. A father-son moment? Do I even want one? It is much easier to have a black-and-white relationship. He's a bad man who thinks of me as a hopeless inconvenience.

Open File: C:\My Files\NGC\hopeless.avi (Date: 7/7/01)

We're at my father's company picnic. I have struck out at all my times at bat in the softball game. I was the first one disqualified in the egg toss. (My partner was my father, who lobbed the egg from one foot away; but I dropped it and ran away when it splattered at my feet.) In the sack races I could not figure out the mechanics of movement, so I fell at the starting line.

I'm sitting by myself at a picnic table eating potato chips when I see my father's boss talking to another man. The Boss is holding a puzzle cube. I slide out of the bench and ask the Boss what it is.

"Rubik's Cube," the Boss says. "It's impossible to solve."

"Can I try it?" I ask. He hands it to me, and I spin the wheels, noticing patterns as colors whirl by. I turn and turn until each side of the cube has one solid color. It takes me two minutes.

"Here." I give the puzzle back to the Boss.

"Holy (R-rated word)!" the Boss says. Then he yells over to my father, who is assembling a hot dog by the barbecue grill.

"Hey, Clark!" The Boss holds up the cube in the air. "Looks like your kid isn't completely hopeless after all!"

Close File.

In the car my father listens to a motivational CD. I try to remain calm. A party. I'm being blackmailed into going to a party.

A suitable analogy? Me : Party :: Earth : Nuclear War. In other words, a catastrophic disaster.

"We're here." My father pulls up at a minimansion indistinguishable from its neighbors. "I'll pick you up at ten thirty. Remember, no drinking, no drugs. Have fun!"

I'm standing out on the sidewalk. Did he just say "drinking" and "drugs"? The last party I attended, my mother warned me about too much soda and sugar. I am not naive. I am aware that teenagers imbibe alcohol and experiment with various forms of drugs. But didn't my father say there would be chaperones?

Thinking about drugs reminds me that I stashed an extra anti-anxiety pill in my jeans pocket. I swallow it without water. It is prescription, as is the Zoloft I take every day for depression, obsessive thinking, and general nervousness.

It occurs to me that I can just take a walk around the neighborhood. Well, several walks. I could fill the time until my father comes back. . . .

"Hey!" The front door of the house opens. "Come on in!"

A boy about my age is yelling to me. I've been spotted. Plan A—walk around the neighborhood—foiled. Plan B: attend the party. I walk up the driveway, which feels as if it's a mile long with an 80-degree incline. Of course it's not. So I make it to the front door and step inside.

TSA! Total sensory assault!

Activate protective shields (which are as imaginary as i, the imaginary number, but are as real to me as i is to complex mathematics)! My invisible shields are meant to reduce noise level, keep a wall between me and others, and block odors.

My shields fail me.

I can hear—and feel—hip-hop music blasting. The room is wall-to-wall people, which means I have total strangers pressing against me as I try to make my way to somewhere less crowded. And the odors? I recognize beer, which my father and Rachel drink occasionally. I am unfamiliar with the sweet, smoky smell in the air, but I can guess what it is. Cannabis.

Must get out. Push, squeeze, excuse me, stumble,

push. . . . I'm in the next room! Unfortunately, it is an interior room. I'm looking for an exit. If I leave I can still tell my father "Yes, I went to the party." For proof I listen carefully to the song that is playing so I can recite its lyrics to my father.

They're misogynistic and profane. Okay, that won't work. I just need to get out of here. My head is swirling, my breathing choppy. I'm going to have a full-blown panic meltdown any second. *PanicPanicPanicPanicPanicPanicPanicPanicPanic*.

"Yo!" Somebody grabs my arm. "Look who's here!"

I'm tugged toward a group of people hanging around a card table. There are no cards. Just cups. And a Ping-Pong ball? You can't play Ping-Pong at a card table, and where are the paddles? Why am I thinking this? Get a grip. Like this guy has a grip on my right arm.

It's Braden. Cooper's video game buddy.

"Hey, everybody," Braden says, still gripping my arm. No way I can escape this muscle guy. At least it's less crowded over here. I catch my breath.

"This is Ed," Braden announces to the table. "Like *Special* Ed."

Please let me out of here, I silently beg the universe. The universe does not respond.

"Braden, that's so mean," a girl seated at the table says. I look at her. She is laughing. She has silver hoops in her nose and eyebrow and a gold ball on her tongue.

"Would you show me the exit?" I have to force myself to speak. I'm shaking with fear and Asperger's.

"Dude," Braden says, "you just got here. I'll be offended if you leave my party already."

His party? This is Braden's house?

"Your father is my father's client," I say, desperate to convince him to let me go. "I just want to—er—thank him for inviting me."

"You want my dad?" Braden says. "Last time I saw him, he was in the kitchen. Hey, go ask him when the pizza's coming."

Braden finally releases my arm.

"I—uh—where's the kitchen?" I'm already moving away from Braden.

"I'll show you, Ed." A blonde girl jumps up from her chair, holding an empty cup. As she walks around the table toward me, she sways and trips over a boy's foot.

"Oopsie," she says. "Ed, catch me." She leans into me. I freeze. A strange girl is touching me!

"Wait," the girl says. "I know you. You're the guy from the bowling alley!"

I search my memory files. Oh. She's the one who ran after her friend called me "hottie." She's not running away now. Huh. She seemed shy then.

"Ashton, this is that guy Piper and I were talking

about," the blonde girl says.

"Ooh, you're right," the pierced girl says. "He *is* like a mashup of Lucas Till and Alex Pettyfer."

"Come on, Ed," the blonde girl says. "Let's go to the kitchen."

She starts leading me away from the table.

"Uh, my name is really Nathaniel," I tell her. If I just hold myself together, I can get out of this madness.

"I'm Mia," she says. "Here's the kitchen. Good, I'm ready for a refill."

I look around—large kitchen—and see a man. Braden's dad. My father's client. I'm about to go over to thank him (for putting me through hell) when I see him pass something to a woman. Something with smoke curling out of it. The woman inhales from it.

The chaperones are smoking marijuana.

And I *still* don't see an exit. I'm trapped!

Could this get any worse?

"Here, Nathaniel," Mia says. "I got you one." She hands me a plastic cup containing a red liquid. I am so sweaty and thirsty, I want to drink it down.

"What is it?" I ask warily.

"Just fruit punch," Mia says. "You don't look like a beer kind of guy." She hiccups, giggles, and takes a long drink from her own cup.

"No thank you," I decide. I look around again for a way out.

And that's when I see her. Dark, bouncy hair, too familiar face—it's Jessa. Leaning against a wall.

Jessa.

Talking to a guy. A guy who reaches out and puts his hand on her shoulder.

I recall Jessa telling me about rule number sixteen. And that if she *were* allowed to date, it might be me.

That guy? Not me.

I look at Jessa again, and all I can think is, *Liar*.

CHAPTER ELEVEN

POSSIBLE SIDE EFFECTS

Q: What is the strength of the gravitational force between two people facing each other? To find the strength of the attraction, use:

$$\frac{f = 4.7e-9 * m_1 m_2}{distance_2}$$

I try to calculate the strength of the attraction between Jessa and the person touching her, but my thoughts and emotions are so muddled, I can't do anything.

Except quench my thirst. I gulp down the fruit punch. Too sweet, but not bad. I'm getting enraged now. I want to confront Jessa.

"Go, Nathaniel!" Mia says. "You chugged that punch!"

Oh. I look back at her. She is quite pretty, in a fair-haired non-Jessa way. She hands me another cup of punch.

"Cheers," she says and clinks her cup against mine. I know the "cheers" protocol and do not want to be rude since Mia is being very kind. So I drink punch along with her, draining the last drop. Then, for a few minutes I just stand there as Mia chats with various people who come over for beverages.

Mia's friend with the piercings comes up to us. I can hear a group of people singing along to a rap song in another room.

"It's your birthday!" they chant.

"Ish it Braden'sh birthday?" I say. "Wazz I shposta bring a presh-a presh-a gift?"

A part of my brain realizes that I'm not speaking right. There must be alcohol in the punch. The medications I am on have adverse reactions when combined with alcohol. Possible effects are mental changes, mood swings, dizziness, confusion, nausea, and vomiting. The other part of my brain is stuck on Jessa and that guy. It doesn't care about what's in the punch. It just wants an escape.

"No, silly." Mia nudges me. I almost fall over and grab the counter to steady myself. "It's just a song."

"Looks like Ed is a lightweight," Pierced Girl comments.

"Not." Mia shakes her head. "He chugs like a rock star. Show 'er, Nathaniel."

I obey.

Then I find myself propped up on Mia instead of the counter. My arm is around her, and she wraps her arms around my waist.

For a brief moment, I am suspended in a moment of pure happiness. So this is what it's like to be accepted by regular teenagers. So this is what a social life is like. Maybe my father was right after all. I just needed to have some fun.

"Nathaniel?" Jessa's voice stabs my bubble. "Are you okay?" She's come over to where I'm hanging out.

"He's fine," Mia says. Her voice is different: sharp, not so giggly. "He's with me."

Mia grabs my head with one hand, pulls it down, and kisses me. On. The. Lips.

Ha! I think wildly. *Take that, Jessa Liar Rose.* I aim a kiss back in Mia's direction. It lands on her neck and leaves a dark red fruit punch imprint.

"Ooh," Pierced Girl squeals. "He's Special *Edward*! Get it, like Edward Cullen? He's marked your neck like a vampire!"

"Blood would have more viscosity," I inform Pierced Girl.

"I've got my own vampire hottie," Mia says, drinking some more punch.

"Nathaniel, I'm going to go get Cooper," Jessa says. "Don't leave. And *don't* drink any more punch. I think Cooper's playing cards upstairs. Be right back."

"Coooop!" I shout. "The Coopshter is here to join our par-tay!"

Jessa disappears.

I raise my fist to yell "par-tay!" again because it is a fun word to say, but I knock Mia's cup out of her hand. It hits the floor, spraying punch on our shoes.

"Oh, fick," I say, looking at the mess.

"It's on my new strappy sandals!" Mia says. "I've gotta go blot it before it stains!" Mia rushes over to the other side of the kitchen where the sinks are. It's a big kitchen.

"Did you just say 'fick'?" Pierced Girl asks me.

It suddenly hits me that I do not feel well.

"Yeh," I mumble, "like Fick's principle, which calculates cardiac output by monitoring oxygen levels in the blood." My words come out in a rush.

"Maybe you are a vampire," Pierced Girl says. "You know entirely too much about blood."

She walks away.

I stand in a puddle of punch.

I do not know what to do.

Then I know exactly what to do. I race across the kitchen, feeling my sneakers sticky, my legs wobbly.

I push Mia away from the sink.

"What the— *Aaah*!" Mia yelps, and backs away.

Vomit. Synonyms: throw up, upchuck, hurl, barf, re-gurgitate, spew . . .

. . . puke.

I do not recall anything after that. No file. No folder. Blackout.

CHAPTER TWELVE
MELTDOWN

x x x x x x x x x x x x x x x x x x x x x x x x x x x x x x x
x x x x x x x x x x x x x x x x x x x x x x x x x x

x x x x x x x x x x x x x x x x x x x x x x x x x x x x x x
x x x x x x x x x x x x x x x x x x x x x x x x x x x

x x x x x x x x x x x x x x x x x x x x x x x x x x x x x x
x x x x x x x x x x x x x x x x x x x x x x x x x x x

x x x x x x x x x x x x x *Nathaniel, open your mouth and drink this water ... can you swallow these aspirin? ... good ...* x x x x x x x x x x x x x x x *aspirin = $C_6H_4COOCH_3COOH$* x x x x x x x x x x x x x x x x x x x
x x x x x x x x x x x x x x x x x x x x x x x x x x x x x x x
x x x x x x x x x x x x

What were you thinking letting him go to that party alone ... just wanted him to have fun ... YOU just wanted ... what about what Nathaniel wants

and more importantly what he needs ... Look, I told Rachel I'd be home as soon as I dropped him off. I've got to get back ... Of course, go run back to your perfect family and leave me to deal with the fallout from your actions as usual ... x x x x x x x x x x x x x x x x
x x x x x x x x x x x x x x x x x x x x x x x x x x x x
x x x x x x x x x x x x x x x x x x x x x x x x x x x x
x x x x x x x x x x x x x x x x x x x x x x x x x x

Hi we can't come to the phone please leave a message ... Mrs. Clark it's Cooper you need to know Nathaniel had no idea there was alcohol in that punch I didn't even know he was at the party can you have him call me thanks ... x x x x x x x x x x x
x x x x x x x x x x x x x x x x x x x x x x x x x x x x x
x x x x x x x x x x x x x x x x x x x x x x x x x x x x x
x x x x x x x x x x x x x

At least three cups ... vodka ... yes I think he vomited it all up ... so the reaction was because of the alcohol and medication combination ... fluids and rest ... thank you, Doctor x x x x x x x x x x x x x x x x
x x x x x x x x x x x x x x x x x x x x x x x x x x x x x
x x x x x x x x x x x x x x x x x

x x x x x x x x x x x x x x x x x x x x x x x x x x x x
x x x x x x x x x x x x x x x x x x x x x x x x x

Hi we can't come to the phone please leave a message ... Nathaniel it's Jessa are you okay please call or

e-mail me ... x x x x x x x x x x x x x x x x x x x x x x x
x x x x x x x x x x x x x x x x x x x x x x x x x x x x x
x x x x x x x x x x x x x x x x x x x x x x x x x x x x x
x x x x x x x x x x x x

Haiku
My head is swimming
In the Lake of Last Night Lost
My mouth tastes like puke

5

7

5

x x x x x x x x x x x x x x x x x x x x x x x x x x x x
x x x x x x x x x x x x x x x x x x x x x x x x
x x x x x x x x x x x x x x x x x x x x x x x x x x x x
x x x x x x x x x x x x x x x x x x x x x x x x
x x x x x x x x x x x x x x x x x x x x x x x x x x x x

x x x x x x x x x x x x x x x x x x x x x x x x x x

x x x x x x x x x x x x x x x x x x x x x x x x x x x x x

x x x x x x x x x x x x x x x x x x x x x x x x x x x

x x x x x x x x x x x x x x x x x x x x x x x x x x x x x

x x x x x x x x x x x x x x x x x x x x x x x x x x x

x x x x x x x x x x x x x x x x x x x x x x x x x x x x x

x x x x x x x x x x x x x x x x x x x x x x x x x x

*Nathaniel, it's Monday time to wake up … sweetie
just open your eyes …* x x x x x x x x x x x x x x x x x

x x x x x x x x x x x x x x x x x x x x x x x x x x x x x x

x x x x x x x x x x x x x x x x x x x x

x x x x x x x x x x x x x x x x x x x x x x x x x x x x x x

x x x x x x x x x x x x x x x x x x x x x x x x x x x

OpenFileCloseFileOpenFileCloseFileOpenFile
CloseFileOpenFileCloseFileOpenFileCloseFile

x x x x x x x x x x x x x x x x x x x x x x x x x x x x x

x x x x x x x x x x x x x x x x x x x x x x x x x x

x x x x x x x x x x x x x x x x x x x x x x x x x x x x x

x x x x x x x x x x x x x x x x x x x x x x x x x x

notageniusstupidhopelessstayinsidewanttohidein-
finiteloopinfinitelooplooplooploop x x x x x x

x x x x x x x x x x x x x x x x x x x x x x x x x x x x x x

x x x x x x x x x x x x x x x x x x x x x x x x x x

1 kilobyte = 1.024 bytes, 1 megabyte =
1,048,576 bytes, 1 gigabyte = 1,073,741,824 bytes,

1 terabyte = 1,099,511,627,776 bytes, 1 petabyte = 1,125,899,906,842,624 bytes . . .

I brought you a bagel—blueberry, your favorite. Just take a bite. x x x x x x x x x x x x x x x x x x x x x x x x x x x x x x x x x x x x x x x x x x x x x x x x x x x x x x x x x x x x x x x x x x x x x x x x

Nathaniel, I understand things got overwhelming for you, but I need you to say something to show me you're . . . there. Okay? Yes or no.

"Yes," I say to my mother, who worries about me but shouldn't because I am fine where I am. Finer than fine. Miner than mine.

Was that a yes? I barely heard you whisper something.

"Yes is the answer to the yes-or-no question," I say. It takes too much effort to speak.

Retreat. Mute mother's voice.

Yes is the answer to a yes-or-no question, but if it is verified in polynomial time, can the solution itself be computed quickly? Does P = NP?

P versus NP, the Hodge Conjecture, the Poincaré Conjecture, the Riemann Hypothesis, the Yang-Mills Theory, the Navier-Stokes Equations, the Birch and Swinnerton-Dyer Conjecture.

Seven problems in mathematics. Called the Millennium Prize Problems. Any person who solves any one of these wins one million dollars. That's right, ladies and gentlemen, one MILLION dollars for one math solution. Only the Poincaré Conjecture has been solved so far, leaving six problems left, that's six lucky golden tickets to mathemillions ...

P = NP. Or does it? The Cook-Levin theorem first proved NP-complete in the Boolean satisfiability problem, but no one since has been able to find a polynomial-time algorithm for that or any subsequent NP-complete problems.

Relativizing proofs, natural proofs, algebrizing proofs—insufficient ...

Nathaniel Gideon Clark breaks through all barriers of proof classification with his stunning new technical approach: Clarkizing! Clarkization is a post-algorithmic technique that may lead to proving or disproving P = NP ...

L I G H T B U L B !

Aha! I can see it! I can see it!

I had been deep at the source of my nothingness when a spectacular event not unlike the Big Bang occurred.

Now all is illuminated.

My physical body is up out of bed and at the

computer, typing furiously. Writing, calculating, rewriting, recalculating, jumping existential orders of logic in a single bound. My mind seems to have a direct connection to the computer's ultimate capabilities, and we convey ideas back and forth in communication beyond the limits to a place we've never been together before . . . the Math-i-verse.

Open File: C:\My Files\n-world.avi (Date: 11/2/06)

"Nathaniel, where do you go when you're not here in our world?" my mother asks.

I think about it.

"I guess it's my world," I say. "N-world."

"Do you go there on purpose," my mom says, "or does it just happen?"

"It depends," I say slowly. It is difficult to think about it, to put it into words. "Sometimes I just end up there, and sometimes I dive in."

"I was just wondering, how do you pull yourself out?" my mom says. "And sometimes I wonder why you come out. You seem happy in your own little world."

"I am," I tell her. "But I'm not really in control over it most of the time. And the more I'm out, the harder it is to stay in."

"You're pretty smart for someone still in the single digits," my mom says. She knows I'm excited that in two months I will be ten years old. "How did I get so lucky to have such an amazing son?"

"May I have something from my Halloween jar?" I ask.

"Go ahead." My mom laughs and leans back on the couch with a book. I jump off the sofa and run to the pantry, where I debate, and then choose a KitKat.

Close File.

I am feeling a rush greater than a sugar buzz. I have transcended into the BIG time. I am a mathematical entity who needs to be known. I deserve to be known.

I must make Clarkization known!

I Google the contact name for the Millennium Prize. No name, but there is an e-mail address. *Well, I did not become a college graduate at the age of fourteen (with a double major) by being passive.*

I type an e-mail.

To whom it may concern:

Attached is a potential lead on solving P = NP. Unfortunately, I did not quite reach any conclusions; but in the event I can offer something of value, I have enclosed my work on Clarkization.

Thank you for your time,

Nathaniel Gideon Clark, BS in Mathematics and Computer Science (age fourteen)

<Attach Document>

<Send>

Clarkization has now been released into the world! It has been freed from my brain and now is en route to whom it may concern! A huge moment in the history of Nathaniel Gideon Clark's march toward genius.

Nathaniel, honey, I'm so happy to see you out of bed.

Hi, Mom. I type. It feels like my only means of communication that is working. Brain to fingertips to keys to computer screen to mother. I wait for her to discover it.

Do you have a sore throat? Do you want some ginger ale? Nathaniel?

No. No. Know. Know. Write what you know. Jessa said, write what you know. What I know could fill 100 gigabytes of computer memory. What I know best is math.

I begin to type again, fingers flying fast and furious.

Nathaniel, I think you might be getting manic. That happened last time Dr. Ali upped your meds. I'm going to give him a call.

I know math I know math I know math I know math. I type math:

To solve equations
Use the order of operations
P.E.M.! D.A.S.!

**Isolate the variable
And solve—oh yes!
Get your algebra on . . .
Get your algebra on!**

Heh.

**Slope—intercept form
y equals mx plus b
A linear equation of the first degree.
A formula graphed on the coordinate plane,
With m as the slope,
A horizontal line's slope zero
Vertical line? Nope, no slope.
I'm bringing algebra back!
All you math haters
Watch while I attack,
The FOIL method—
Quadratic equations are a fact
Of high school life, and must be passed—
So remember *First Out In* and *Last*—
And get your algebra on!**

I continue typing faster and faster. Linear inequalities. Types of functions. All in the form of a song.
Then I'm done.

I save it in a folder I title "Algebra in Verse." In Verse. Inverse. Appropriate for my life, which has turned upside down.

Math is still swirling around in my brain, so I move on to "Geometry in Verse." Principles and proofs. Plane figures and solids. Transformations. Formulas . . . all pour out of my brain onto the paper.

Open File: C:\My Files\band\songs\Jessa.avi (Date 9/30/10)
"That's what songwriters do." Jessa grins. "They write about what they know and pour their heart out on the page."
Close File.

Close heart.

Algebra and geometry in verse? That's what mathwriters do. They pour their brains out onto the page.

Nathaniel, stop typing. You need to eat. Here is a bagel. Eat. Good. Drink this juice. Good. Dr. Ali said that you're eating and drinking is a positive sign. I brought you a brownie, too, for when you want it. Now listen. Dr. Ali is calling in a prescription for you. Your father is picking it up and bringing it over here.

My mind is racing. Mania: a condition that is characterized by excessive energy, accelerated mental activity, and emotional instability.

Mania? Compulsion? Obsession? Whatever. I cannot stop my brain from dumping academic knowledge into the computer in verse form. I am energized!

Energy. That's physics. That's what science writers do.

Basic Physics
Physics makes our world rock and roll.
May its forces be with you like Jedi mind control.
Over objects in motion and objects at rest.
Yoda may be the master, but Sir Isaac said it best.
An object in motion will remain in motion
Unless acted upon by an outside force.
An object keeps moving 'til something stops it—
Newton's First Law of Motion, of course.
An object at rest will remain at rest,
Inertia's a property couch potatoes know best
So get off your a*s, you lazy mass.
Let physics rock your world!
Energy's defined in terms of work,
W equals f times d.
When a force moves through distance d,
It causes a release of energy.
Force overcomes inertia,
Newton's Second Law states,
Press down on the gas pedal and accelerate.

F equals *m* times *a*, so don't drive too fast.
Newton's Third Law of Motion explains a car crash.
Action equals reaction, so if you hit a tree,
Equal but opposite forces can cause a tragedy
So may the forces be with you,
'cause they rule our galaxy . . .

I'm typing so fast my fingers blur. I add verses about electricity, magnetism, and mechanics. Yes. Basic physics is finished. *Physicsphysicsphysicsphysphysfizzfizz*—

That brain loop makes me think of chemistry. Think I'll do that next.

Chemical reactions, molarity, stoichiometry, the periodic table . . . all flow fluidly into a test tube of typed text.

Next up? Trig/precalculus. Trigonometry goes so easily, precalculus is so obvious. That verse practically writes itself.

Nathaniel, your father's here. I'm going to go take a nap.

Nathaniel, this is your father speaking. Snap out of it.

The next logical verse would be calculus or biology. But I'm a little calc'd out, and I've never been that interested in studying living things.

So, let's go, particle physics!

At least take this pill. Your doctor says it will calm you down. You know what would calm you down? A kick in the pants, that's what. Or how about if I unplug this computer . . . okay, okay. I won't—stop freaking out, Nathaniel! I won't touch it. Jeez.

It is fun to write a verse about the "particle zoo" and its inhabitants: hadrons and leptons, baryons and mesons, muons and gluons—the smallest bits of matter and energy that exist.

I take a detour and decide to invent my own imaginary particle: the aspon.

Characteristics of the ASPON:

- sensitive to fast movements and loud noises
- does not interact easily with other particles
- occasionally reacts with quantum weirdness

I've invented particle me!

Nathaniel, listen to me. Your mother and I agree that you need to come off the computer. I'm going to save your work and shut down. We need to talk about that party. . . .

Partypartybobartybananafanafofarty . . .

Party.

Braden's party.

No! Don't bring that horribleterribleawfulness into my safe place. No, oh no! Please . . . no . . .

Open File: C:\My Files\BradenParty_1.avi (Date 10/12/10)
The crowd of sweaty, perfumey bodies . . . the panicky need for fresh air . . . can't find the way out . . . sweet fruit punch . . . strange girl's lips . . . help I'm gonna' be sick . . .
Close File.

I cannot get back to the present; I am trapped in the past. Suddenly everything catches up to me like a tsunami, a hurricane through my brain—*Open-FileOpenFileOpenFileOpenFile*—as if a tornado is blowing through at a twelve on the TORRO International Tornado Intensity Scale, total devastation, and although I'm gripping on so hard,

I

am being

swept away.

Nathaniel? My father sounds far away, as if he is at the end of a tunnel. A familiar tunnel.

The computer is off. My connection to the real world is also shut off. I slide deeper into the void, and I feel a sudden sense of rightness. Comfort. It is the place of my childhood, my escape, my N-world. The autistic part of my brain is a seductress, tempting me with the siren song of bliss.

Really, N-world is the only place for me. It is all I need.

CHAPTER THIRTEEN
THINK AGAIN

THAT'S A LOAD OF BS.

Who said that? Why are there voices in my head? Am I schizophrenic?

YOU'RE NOT SCHIZOPHRENIC.

Who is saying that?

ME.

An avatar appears in my mental picture. It looks exactly like me.

I AM YOU. IN N-WORLD.

I am disturbed. The point of N-world is that there is no human-bodied Me; there is just my mind that is able to float freely.

YOU AREN'T FREE IF YOU'RE TRAPPED IN-SIDE YOUR OWN HEAD.

I tune him out. There is no place for logic in N-world.

Andrea! I need a little help in here.

I turn my attention to the music. It is as if the mythical mermaids are lulling me, soothing me. I am a hero of Greek mythology, mesmerized by the sirens of the sea. My ship rocks back and forth and . . .

THINK AGAIN. THOSE AREN'T MYTHICAL MERMAIDS SINGING. IT'S YOU. YOU ARE HUMMING. AND THE SHIP ISN'T ROCKING—YOU ARE.

For an instant I can see what the outer world can see: me sitting, rocking back and forth and humming.

Oh, for crap's sake, Nathaniel. I watch my father watch *me* rock and hum.

Whoosh . . . back into my own N-world. Which is still being invaded by mini-Me. Now he has a laptop. My avatar has *my* laptop.

NOW, TO GET THESE FILES BACK IN ORDER . . . MOVE FILE. MOVE FILE. RENAME FILE FOLDER . . .

I can feel my brain reorganizing itself, files spinning like a Rubik's Cube returning to its original form, all colors united.

Suddenly, the avatar dumps a file into a Recycle Bin. *Hey!!!! You can't do that! Get away! Go away!* I try to knock him out of my head. This is a nightmare! Both

N-world and the real world have been invaded. Unwelcome, uninvited intruders. Get out!

Andrea! My father is back. Alone. *We have a situation! Nathaniel, stop hitting yourself in the head. Stop. Right now. Ugh, this is a nightmare!*

My father is not leaving. This avatar is not leaving. What file did he throw out? It had better not be math related. . . .

I THREW OUT THE BRADENPARTY_GUILTY. AVI FILE. EVERYONE HAS SAID YOU'VE DONE NOTHING WRONG. SO NO MORE POST-PARTY-TRAUMATIC STRESS. DELETE.

I have a file named BradenParty_ guilty.avi? When did I create that?

WHEN YOU WERE BLACKOUT DRUNK, YOUR CONSCIOUS MIND WAS NON-FUNCTIONAL, BUT YOUR SUBCONSCIOUS RECORDED EVERYTHING FROM THAT NIGHT. NOW, WHERE IS THAT BRADENPARTY_JESSA.AVI FILE?

I don't want to see that! I don't even want it. Delete it!

AHA! HERE IT IS. I WILL LEAVE IT RIGHT HERE FOR WHEN YOU ARE READY TO OPEN IT.

Didn't you hear me? I don't want to see it! (I am

getting tired. N-world has never been so complicated, so out of my control.)

LIFE IS OUT OF YOUR CONTROL. ENJOY!

The avatar disappears with a pop, like a bubble.

Enjoy what? Being confused? I mentally observe the file the avatar left behind, but I do not open it. It obviously happened, because I stored and filed it, because it is in *my* memory.

But that does not mean I want to replay it, to relive it. I just want to sleep.

Nathaniel, listen to us. This is serious. My mother is back in my room.

Dr. Ali says if you do not come in to see him for an appointment right now, he will send an ambulance to take you to the psychiatric ward of the hospital.

Uh . . . huh?

I don't think so!

I've had enough of N-world today, anyway. The music, the rocking—all stopped. There are no visuals, no numbers, no activities. Just blankness. I begin to feel a little claustrophobic. Time to go back out.

Going. Back. Out. . . . My self is being sucked out of the crevice of my brain, where I've been, where so much has happened.

Illumination! Brain dump verses! Avatar intruder!

Done. I sever the connection to N-world. I close

my eyes and let the reintegration process complete itself.

"Erggh. . . ," I groan, opening my eyes and shutting them again. Real-life sunshine is much harsher than a lightbulb of the mind.

"It's too bright in here, Mom. I wish I had window shades made of nanoscale filaments."

"Sure, honey," my mom says. "I'll search for some on eBay as soon as we get back from seeing Dr. Ali."

"What are you two talking about?" my father says. "Are we taking him to the hospital or not?"

"Not," I say firmly.

I sit up and stretch. I feel like half Nathaniel and half empty shell. I reluctantly begin my reentry into the NT world.

"Go home, Steven," my mother says. "Thank you for your help." Then she comes over and gives me a too-tight hug and bursts into tears.

Soon after, my mother pulls herself together and drives me to my doctor's appointment.

"It's good to see you," Dr. Ali says to my mother, then whisks me off to his private office.

I take my usual seat on the reclining chair, but I do not recline. The velvety feel of the armrests soothes me. I stare at the diplomas and certificates and awards on the wall. I have memorized them over the five years and two months I have been coming here. It's good to see that none of them has been taken down or rearranged.

"So, you had a bad weekend, Nathaniel?" Dr. Ali asks. He has a musical Indian accent I like. Since I've been seeing him, my height has gone from reaching his shoulder to me being five inches taller. Although his stature has diminished comparatively, my respect for him has grown.

Still, that does not mean I plan to talk to him about what happened. I never plan to talk about what happened.

"What happened?" Dr. Ali prompts.

"How was *your* weekend?" I ask. Perhaps I can turn the conversation with my social skills.

"Fine, thank you," Dr. Ali says. "And yours?"

I shut my mouth and focus on the recliner's material. When I run my finger up one way, it looks paler; and when I run it back down, the pale line seems erased.

Minutes tick by.

"Okay, Nathaniel," Dr. Ali finally says. "You don't have to talk about the weekend. I've known you a long time, and you've never had such an intense break from reality. But you came back when you decided to. So I commend you on your awareness and good judgment. I don't believe it was a psychotic break or I'd have to recommend inpatient therapy. Can you promise me that you will try not to retreat into yourself when you get back home?"

"If the alternative is lockdown and enforced therapeutic interventions, then yes, I will do my best to participate in what is known as the real world," I grumble.

"Do you have any urge to hurt yourself?" Dr. Ali asks.

"No," I tell the doctor.

"Do you have any urge to hurt others?"

"No."

"Have you had any thoughts of suicide this past week?" Dr. Ali keeps going.

"No."

"I believe you, Nathaniel." He nods and writes down some things on a pad of paper.

"I'm going to call in your mother so we can come up with a daily plan," Dr. Ali says. "But, Nathaniel? First, can you tell me—when you were somewhere inside yourself—what was there that the world doesn't offer you?"

"Honesty." I flip up my hoodie and pull the strings tight. "Truth." Then I yank the strings closed to make my face disappear.

I hear Dr. Ali invite my mother into the office. She

comes in, but I stay in my hood retreat.

"Okay, Mrs. Clark, I'm going to allow Nathaniel to try being home. I think this is an aberration rather than something more ominous. Still, I'm writing a list of things that Nathaniel will need to do every day— non-negotiable. I'll have my assistant make a copy for Nathaniel's father also."

"Thank you so much, Dr. Ali." My mom exhales loudly.

"Make an appointment for one week from today," Dr. Ali says. "But call me anytime, even if it's not an emergency. We need to stay on top of things, so do not hesitate to contact me.

"Nathaniel, your mother will make sure you follow your daily list. Are you hearing me?" I don't mess with Dr. Ali. I pull off my hood.

"Yes, Dr. Ali," I say.

He leaves the office for two minutes and forty-five seconds and returns with two sheets of paper, which he gives to my mom.

In the elevator, my mother shows me one paper.

NATHANIEL CLARK

(med)	Increase Zoloft by 25 mg/day
(exercise)	At least one 15-minute walk outside daily
(self-care)	Daily shower and grooming

(social)	Speak to at least one non-family member per day (phone or in person)
(nutrition)	One multivitamin, one Omega 3-6-9 capsule, balanced diet—plenty of fruits, vegetables, whole grains, and protein

"Okay," I say. My legs and head feel so heavy, I can't imagine doing all that. I just want to sleep. As soon as I buckle myself in the car, I fall asleep.

"Wakey, wakey." My mother's voice interrupts my nap. "We're home."

"Zerghk," I say, meaning "I'm trying to sleep here."

"You need to take your fifteen-minute walk," she says, bright and cheerful. I slump farther down in my seat.

Tune out ignore tune out ignore tune ...

"Ow!" I yelp, jumping up from my seat. "Ow!" I yell again after hitting my head on the car's interior roof. (I keep forgetting I am six feet tall now.)

"You hit me," I say to my mother. "You're the one who needs to be locked up, you crazy, violent woman."

"I hit you with an empty water bottle," my mom replies. "That hardly constitutes abuse."

"Fine." I unbuckle and get out of the car. "I'll walk." The water bottle didn't really hurt, just surprised me.

Still. The top of my head throbs a tiny bit. I walk, slowly at first. I breathe in the crisp, autumn air. Leaves crunch under my feet. I head down the street, where there are fewer houses and more lawn.

I'm in the more woodsy area of the neighborhood. I hear a *rat-tat-tat* and look up at a tree to see a red-bellied woodpecker. Gray squirrels race away as I come near. When I was younger, I was forced to play outside. My mom said she was treating my nature deficit disorder. That time outside certainly did give me plenty of opportunities to experience the natural world.

I never learned to like it. Give me a climate-controlled room any day.

"Be-beep! Be-beep!" I raise my arm and turn off the timer on my watch. Seven minutes and thirty seconds. I'd set it to go off when it was time for me to turn around. Time = rate/distance. I would get back home in exactly fifteen minutes.

At exactly fourteen minutes and three seconds, I'm rounding the curve to home. I've reached the bottom of my driveway when I hear an unwelcome sound.

"Nathaniel! Hey, hold up!" It's Cooper.

2 4 6 8 10 12 14 16 18 20 22 steps to the open garage door. I scoot in, hitting the Down button on the auto-door device on my way into the house. Cooper disappears.

I celebrate the near miss with my own version of a cheer: "Three Quarks for Nathaniel Clark . . . Go, Me!"

Too bad there isn't a pep squad to cheer for physicists. I'll bet Einstein would have enjoyed that.

$E=mc^2$

Your team is worse than Albert's hair!

I walk upstairs. Whew. I'm exhausted.

Back to my room. Back to bed.

CHAPTER FOURTEEN

HOW DID A LOBOTOMIZED CHIMP GET IN HERE?

I roll over in bed, preparing to enjoy a long, slow awakening.

"It's about time," a voice says from nearby.

"Aaah!" I sit upright. Cooper is sitting in my computer chair with his feet up on my desk.

"Dude, I've been waiting for you to wake up forever," he says. "It's time to come out of the Batcave and into the light."

"Huh?" I look at the clock. 9:52 a.m.

"You're coming over to my house," Cooper announces. "A little foosball, some Wii kick-butt games, maybe a movie on the HD big-screen . . . the entertainment options are endless."

I had planned another day in. I do not change plans easily. I will have to get rid of Cooper. But I am still half asleep, so I try to focus on focusing on Plan Go Cooper. (An evil plot? No, I don't do evil well.) I have to consider *his* life. School, friends, the mundane priorities of a regular teen.

"Don't you need to get to school?" I say.

"Teacher in-service," Cooper responds. "Day off."

"Well, what about your friends?" I say.

"I was too lazy to make plans," Cooper says, "but I'm not as lazy as you—sleepmaster."

"Is your plan to insult me so I go over to your house?" I grumble.

"Whatever works," Cooper says. "So, tag, you're It, my friend. Get up and let's do it!"

I'm out of bed, yawning and stumbly.

"Nice jammies," Cooper says.

"They're comfortable," I retort. So what if they're a bright yellow SpongeBob SquarePants matching set? "Besides, nobody asked you to come over and see them. Look, Cooper, I am in the middle of a project, so I can't go over to your house."

"What, is this project so important you can't spend a few hours away from it?" Cooper yawns. "Are you solving the economic crisis? World peace? Or something else to prove that you're a genius?"

I have no logical comeback. I haven't solved anything. Especially my non-genius situation.

($N \neq G$) = *Ugghhh* + *Aaaack*. I don't even have a logical formula to explain my inability to prove why I am not a genius yet. I am not fit for the outside world.

"None of the above," I confess. "I just don't want to go out. The world is like a stupid field of land mines just waiting for me to step on them and blow myself up."

"Well . . . there's a land mine–free zone stretching between my house and yours," Cooper says. "Just come over, bring your project, and I'll have Anna make those pancakes you like."

Anna, the Owens' cook-housecleaner, makes the best pancakes, with chunks of melted chocolate. Mmmm . . . chocolate.

"Okay," I say. "You win."

"Good," Cooper answers. "Because you lost me back there with that land-mine talk. Although I think I covered up quite well, don't you? Toss a load of bullsh** into an argument and hope the other guy slips in it. That's what my dad says."

"So, you wanted me to fall in rhetorical poop to vanquish me?" I am now losing my place in this conversation.

"Buddy." Cooper sighs. "I just want you to come over to my house. I'm pretty sure I heard a yes somewhere in there, so I'll see you at my place in a few."

Cooper moonwalks backward out of my room.

It is so difficult to relate to my peers. I wish they came with a handbook, although it would be easier if they didn't come at all.

Ten minutes later I'm ringing Cooper's doorbell. "Nathaniel!" Cooper opens the door with a look I can't interpret. "What a pleasant surprise! What brings you to my neck of the woods?"

"Uh—er— Didn't you ask me— Wasn't I supposed to—," I sputter, wondering if I misinterpreted his invitation.

"Joking," Cooper says. "Get in here. Anna's whipping up breakfast."

"Technically, it's brunch," I inform him.

"Technically, it's food," Cooper says. "So let's eat."

We're finishing our third helping of pancakes. Cooper swallows some orange juice.

"You know, you weren't the only one to upchuck at the party Saturday night," he says.

The pancake feels like lead going down my throat. I don't want to talk about this. I don't even want to think about this!

"Yeah, Elana Fitch lost it all over the beer-pong table," Cooper continues, "and this lacrosse kid passed out on the front lawn. I heard they're okay, too, just like you."

I'm not okay! I'm not okay about anything!

"At least you made it to the sink," Cooper says. "Don't let it get to you. Everyone knows you didn't drink liquor on purpose. Even your dad was pretty cool about it when we called him to pick you up."

"'We who' called my dad?" I ask, startled. "You talked to my father? He saw me all drunk?"

How come I remember nothing of this?

"Jessa and me," Cooper says. "You don't remember? We took you outside and waited with you until your father came. Nice Lexus, by the way. He let you drive it ever?"

My head is swimming.

"My father picked me up?" I repeat. "What did he say? What did *I* say?"

"Oh, we told your dad it was totally not your fault," Cooper assures me, "but he kept apologizing for you, saying *you* couldn't help embarrassing yourself."

"What a jerk," I grumble.

"Yeah, that's what you said then, too," Cooper says. "It was classic."

"Oh, great." I groan. "I called him a jerk in front of everyone?"

"Just in front of us, your friends," Cooper tells me. "And we were all on your side, saying it was just drunk talk, and really you didn't mean anything and don't be mad. I think your dad bought it, 'cause he calmed down.

Then you just kind of fell into your father's car, and that was pretty much that."

Well. I was still embarrassed, but I guess it could have been worse.

"Oh, except when you called Jessa a liar just before your father came," Cooper adds. "I think you said, 'Liar, liar, pants on fire.' It was totally random."

Now that's worse. My hand starts hitting myself in the head. Stupid! Stupid! Stupid!

"Hey." Cooper grabs my hand. "Stop autisticking out. After you left, Jessa wasn't mad or anything. She just wanted you to be okay."

Sure, and then she skipped back into the party, into the arms of her boyfriend, breaking rule number sixteen and my hopes and dreams ...

"Anyways, we've got band practice tomorrow," Cooper says. "We can talk it out then if you need to."

"No!" I yelp. "No more talking about it. It's over. Delete. Erase from all memory."

"Sure, whatever," Cooper says.

I look at him out of the corner of my eye. His brown hair is spiky and shiny. He is three inches shorter than I am but I'll bet that hair adds an extra three-quarters of an inch. Prickly porcupine.

It occurs to me that Cooper is a very good friend.

"Did you know that Sonic the Hedgehog can roll so

fast, he becomes a blur? That's velocity beyond any land mammal!" I tell him.

"Is that a Wii challenge?" Cooper asks.

"No," I answer. "But *this* is: bowling, three games; and I'll give you a ten-point handicap."

As much as I stink at sports, Wii sports are different. Especially bowling. I rule the Wii bowling alley.

"You're on," Cooper says. "I'm feeling lucky, got my A game today. N-dog, you're going down."

"Down the lane into the strike zone," I retort.

And we head off toward the entertainment room, making our way through the maze that is the Owens' mini-mansion.

"Oooh, yeah, that's the way I like it!"

We enter the room to find two little girls jumping and singing into Wii microphones.

"Crap," says Cooper. "It's karaoke. Claire, get out. Go play with some Barbies or something."

Claire is Cooper's younger sister. She is always at school or some activity, so I tend to forget she exists.

"Nuh-uh," Claire says. "Me and Megan were here first; and if you bug us, I'll text Daddy on you."

"'I'll text Daddy on you,'" Cooper says in a mocking tone. If *I* had said it, it would be called echolalia. But when Cooper says it to Claire, it's called sibling rivalry.

"Let's go," Cooper says. I follow him upstairs to the

family room, where we each sit on a leather couch layered with silk cushions. *Aaah*...textures.

"So, ya gonna show me what's on that thing or what?" Cooper asks.

"What thing?" I say, spacing out on the sensations.

"The laptop you've been carrying around with you all morning," my friend says. "What's on it: national secrets? Did you hack into a government Web site and find out they're hiding aliens? Or track down a terrorist cell using your genius encryption code breaking? Or—"

"Stop!" I say. "It's nothing. It's the opposite of intelligence. It's just dumb stuff."

"Then I can understand it!" Cooper says. "Finally I can look at something you've done without feeling like a lobotomized chimp."

"A what?" I look at Cooper.

"I saw it on some late-night old-time movie," Cooper says. He gets up, hunches over, and swings his arms monkey-style. He sticks out his tongue and says, "Duhhh . . . I'm a chimp with no brains. . . . Where are my brains?" He jumps up on my couch and starts poking me.

"What's your problem?" I shrink away.

"Checking for fleas," Cooper says. Then he pokes my hair. "Looking for brains."

"You're insane." I leap off the couch. My brain flips

a switch, and my sense of humor kicks in. I start laughing. A lobotomized chimpanzee . . . hunting for brains. That *is* funny.

I trip on a knocked-over cushion and land on the floor, where I lie back and laugh.

Cooper's laughing too. He's also booting up my laptop. He types in my user name: mathboy14.

"Password?" he asks.

I get serious immediately and get up off the floor.

CHAPTER FIFTEEN

AND THIS IS GREAT . . . WHY, EXACTLY?

"**G**ive me that." I grab my laptop. "Nobody knows my password. Security will never be breached."

I type in my password: ********.

"Okay, promise not to laugh," I say, resigned to Cooper seeing my brain dump material.

"What's this? Algebra?" Cooper mutters. He is silent as he reads and scrolls and reads and scrolls down farther.

My leg starts bouncing up and down and jiggling. I bite the inside of my lip. Why is my body acting so agitated? This is no big deal.

"Nathaniel!" Cooper startles the heck out of me.

"What?" I say. "What?"

"This is amazing!" Cooper exclaims.

"It's just algebra," I say. "I was doing algebra when I was seven. It's just basic stuff."

"Dude, you wrote song lyrics for math?" Cooper starts laughing.

"You promised not to laugh," I say. "Give me back my laptop! Give it! Give it!"

Cooper is not giving it.

"Nathaniel, calm down and listen to me!" Cooper pushes me away. "Calm. Breathe in. Breathe out. Good, now listen to me."

I'm gritting my teeth, but I'm listening.

"Your song lyrics are really good! I was actually interested in ALGEBRA for a minute!" Cooper yells.

"Well, I guess that is good," I respond. "And loud, by the way."

"You're not getting it," Cooper says. "If we come up with some music for this—nothing fancy, just a good melody and a bangin' beat—we can have a great song."

"And this is great . . . why exactly?" I ask.

"Because most of us regular people don't learn algebra when we are seven!" Cooper's voice is rising again. "And most of us regular people don't like it! No one expects algebra to be fun. We suffer for months—years even—while we're teenagers. It's killing some of the best years of our lives!"

"You are quite dramatic," I observe. But I'm starting to catch on.

"Plus, it'll be great exposure for our band!" Cooper says. "Algebra for peace!"

"I also have geometry," I say.

This shuts up Cooper. I take the computer and open the file for "Geometry in Verse." Then I show him trig/precalc and calculus. By the time I get to physics and chemistry, Cooper's grabbed a pad of paper and is writing down things.

I zone and begin to replay an episode of *The Big Bang Theory* from season two, where Sheldon goes to the Renaissance Faire as Spock, scouting out historical inaccuracies.

"Hello, McFly?" Cooper says in my ear.

"What!" I snap out of it.

"We are going to record these songs and put them on YouTube," Cooper announces. "The combination of your information and our killer music will be so cool! Math and music!"

"We'll be mathemusicians." I think about it. "Okay, I guess. If you really want to."

"Yeah, I want to." Cooper pops up from the couch and pulls an iPhone from its charging dock. "I'm going to text Jessa and Logan and get them over here."

"No!" I react instinctively, laying down the laptop and leaping toward Cooper. I slam into him, we both hit the ground, and the iPhone spurts out of Cooper's hand. It skids a few feet away. I lie on the carpet face-down. Cooper slides himself away from me. He sits up, rubbing his shoulder.

"I—" I'm not sure what to say. "I'm—I just think we need a little more time to think about this."

A *lot* more time.

#1) I was not prepared to leave my house today.

#2) I was not prepared to have my personal project, which was meant to *tune out life*, force me *into* a social setting.

#3) I was not prepared to face Jessa, the girl who broke her parents' rules and lied to my face.

"Maybe next month?" I suggest. I spit out a carpet fuzz that got in my mouth. Yech. Time to sit up.

"No way," Cooper says. I glance at him. He's shaking his head from side to side. His hair spikes don't move.

"I've got an algebra midterm next week," Cooper says. "My algebra teacher called me 'hopeless' after the last quiz. I *need* this song to pump me up. To shake off some of my nerves."

"Oh." I realize I need to be a good friend. It's my turn. But is there a way to do this without Jessa?

Open File: C:\My Files\range_rover.avi (Date 2/12/00)

"I'm Superman!" the kid says. "You want to be Batman or Spider-Man?"

Close File.

Open File: C:\My Files\CooperOwens_1.avi (Date: 9/19/00)

"I'm Anakin!" Cooper says. "Who are you? Luke Skywalker or Darth Vader?"

Close File.

Open File: C:My Files\CooperOwens_2.avi (Date: 3/31/01)

"I'm Tarzan of the Jungle!"

Close File.

Open File: C:\My Files\CooperOwens_3.avi (Date: 12/9/02)

"I'm Jack Sparrow!"

Close File.

"How about," I venture, "I be Max Planck and you be Einstein?"

That felt really awkward. My first attempt to play "pretend" is at age fourteen and three-quarters.

"What?" Cooper says.

I guess I did not perform the social ritual correctly.

"I will be Planck; you be Einstein," I clarify.

"What?" Cooper repeats. This is wearing out my patience.

"Planck was a physicist famous for his foundational work in quantum theory." I sigh. "He played musical duets with Einstein. Planck on piano, Einstein on violin."

I wait for Cooper to get psyched. I give up waiting pretty quickly.

"I'll be on keyboard like Planck, and you're on strings like Einstein," I say. "You know, on your guitar? Strings?"

"Um," Cooper says. "No."

Darn.

"Let's forget about those physics guys," he says. "And think about us. You and me playing the songs? Fine. But what about the lyrics? As gifted as you are in many ways, Nat, your voice is simply not as appealing as the lovely and talented Jessa's."

He has a point.

"And I don't think Logan would appreciate being called 'unnecessary,'" Cooper continues. "Unless zero *is* just a zero."

"Fine!" I say. "Text them." I would just find a way to deal with Jessa's presence. I am officially on the autistic spectrum; it should be natural for me to tune out people.

Cooper sends his texts, and unfortunately both Logan and Jessa are available this afternoon. I decide to go home for lunch and come back for our band session. Cooper says he's going to work on the tune for the algebra song.

"I'm impressed with your work ethic," I say.

"It's more like revenge," Cooper says. "No teacher insults me and gets away with it!"

"Did she really call you hopeless?" I ask.

"Yeah, and my grandmother says I'm an incompetent trust-fund slacker," Cooper says in a low voice.

Ouch. Whose grandmother insults them? I feel a small fire ignite inside me. "What is wrong with your family?" I ask.

"Oh, we've been dysfunctional for generations. Actually, I think it's tough love. My grandmother's plan is to shame me into success."

"Don't worry," I tell him. "We'll do that song, I'll help you study, and you will ROCK that test!"

"That's right!" Cooper cheers up. "Rock and roll!" He jumps and makes his hands shake with his fingers stuck out like horns.

"Math with the devil!" he howls.

"Please, no satanic references," I remind him. Devil references are inappropriate in my moral framework. The Grim Reaper is also off-limits, but that's because he scares the jeepers out of me.

"Sorry," Cooper says. I leave him strumming an air guitar, singing "'Algebra . . . wears a bra.' Oh, yeah, math is so sexy!"

And I am supposed to be the weird one.

CHAPTER SIXTEEN
ALL HATERS, CLEAR THE DANCE FLOOR

Back home in my kitchen. I microwave mac 'n' soy cheese, pour myself a glass of organic apple juice, and sit down for lunch. My mom comes in with a load of tote bags. She must have been grocery shopping.

"Thank you for the note you left," Mom says. "It was a nice surprise to see you went to Cooper's house."

"It wasn't exactly my idea," I tell her.

"I know," Mom says. "I let him in this morning."

"Oh."

I watch my mother unload items from the bags.

"You had us worried there for a little while," Mom says. "How are you doing today? I know it's hard for you to put your feelings into words, Nathaniel, but can you give me a little idea?"

I eat for a moment and then swallow. Mom is busy organizing a cabinet. It's easier to think and converse when she is not entirely focused on me.

"I am on autopilot," I say. "I am behaving more acceptably, but I cannot fully connect my actions with my N-self, which is short for 'Nathaniel-self,' who is the person I am when I am aligned with my truth. Also, I still feel a little hungry. May I have some of those chips?"

"I guess it's *not* so hard for you to put your feelings into words," my mother says, raising one eyebrow. Mom tosses me the bag of baked potato chips. I struggle a moment, then the two sides of the bag peel apart and the *poof* of potato chip scent reaches my nose. Mmmm . . . chips.

"So, it was interesting when your father dropped you off drunk Saturday night," Mom says, rearranging some cans on a higher shelf.

"I don't want to talk about it," I say. I start crunching the chips loudly.

"I am sure you don't," my mother says, "but we have to. There are a lot of lessons to be learned from this."

I groan and crunch.

"Which we won't get into now," Mom continues, "but soon. Right now I just want to say that I'm glad you are safe. And I'm proud that you have Cooper and Jessa, two friends you can trust."

One friend singular, I amend but not out loud.

"Nathaniel." My mom sighs. "You are an incredible person. People compliment me all the time on what a well-mannered, nice son I have. And you know some people do not believe you have Asperger's syndrome because you have friends and behave well."

"That's because they don't see me at home," I say, "when I am myself."

"And I *do* see you at home," Mom says, "in all your Aspie glory. That is the reason I've always given you hours of downtime, by yourself, with the freedom to *be* yourself. I hoped that would de-stress you and give you the energy you'd need for when you went out and socialized with others. And all those hours of work behind the scenes . . . very few people have seen the whole picture. You and I and Dr. Ali, and your old therapists, and Grandma—*we* all know how much effort has been put into teaching you the skills to engage with the world."

"Yeah, I agree." Ever since my memory files were created, I have added thousands of neurotypical facts, skills, and behaviors that have been taught to me. Nothing the world seems to think is important has come naturally. I've had to work at it.

"The hardest thing, though . . . " My mom closes the cabinet doors, sits down at the table, and takes a chip.

"The hardest thing has been getting you to *want* to engage with the world. I've had to convince you that being out here with *us* is worth the effort when I know that being in your head, alone, is so much easier. And probably more fun."

"More fun than that party, *that's* for sure," I say, and smile a little.

"What's that?" My mother makes an exaggerated shocked face. "Was that a sense of humor I just glimpsed?"

"Mom," I respond, "you can't *glimpse* verbal humor. Duh! You can *hear* a joke or *glimpse* something visual that is funny. So your usage of the word 'glimpse' was inaccurate—"

"Glimpse this," my mother interrupts, and throws a potato chip at me. It bounces off my nose.

"You have been increasingly violent lately," I say. I am only teasing her now. "I refuse to stoop to your level."

"'Stoop,'" my mom says. "'Glimpse.' 'Stoop.' Those are the silliest-sounding words. Try to say them five times fast."

"Glimpsestoopglimpsestoopglimstoo . . ." I start mangling the words almost immediately. My mom and I take turns glimpse-stooping and laughing. Finally, I need to take a breather.

"Mom?" I say after catching my breath. "Maybe the

reason you worked so hard to engage me in the real world is to give me a choice. So that when I am independent, *I* can decide how much time and energy I will put toward my real-world goals. I will *always* have my N-world. You've just given me more options that I would not have known about—or been able to handle as well—if you hadn't shown me the way."

Silence

Silence

Sniffle

"Excuse my manners, my brilliant, wonderful son. I am very touched by what you just said." My mom reaches for a napkin. She blows her nose into it.

"You just bought a three-pack of tissues," I point out. "I saw you stack them in the pantry."

My mother just smiles and sniffs and takes another napkin to blow into.

"Okay." I shrug. "It's your nose. Tissues are much less abrasive, not to mention less expensive per unit; but if you want to make the wrong choice, I can't stop you."

My mother makes me go to her for a kiss before I walk back over to Cooper's house.

"Love you," she says as I'm leaving. I look back at her and see that she's gotten up and gone into the pantry. I watch her rip into the tissues. I can relax a tiny bit, knowing that my mother—and her nose—will be okay.

Halfway between my house and Cooper's house, I get a reality check. Sharon's car is backing out of the driveway. She honks and waves at me, smiling. I wave back. My mother's BF.

Poor woman. She has no idea what her daughter is really up to.

And then—hello! I remember I am about to face said daughter! What am I going to do? I race through my mental file folder labeled COMMUNICATION. Flipping through the cards, I pass INITIATE A CONVERSATION, KEEP THE CONVERSATION GOING, and reach KEEP A CONVERSATION SHORT. I picture that card (originally made by my mother during social skills lessons) and read: **Be polite. If you are not interested in the topic or do not feel comfortable talking to the person, say "Excuse me, I need to get a drink of water" or other reasonable action.**

I march up to Cooper's house as if going into battle (metaphor: figurative language). I enter the house, make my way to the war room (aka music garage), and stand in the doorway.

"Nathaniel!" Cooper looks up from some papers.

"Whaddup?" says Logan, already seated behind his drum set.

"Hi, Nathaniel!" Jessa comes running over to me and gives me a hug.

Sneak attack! Unexpected!

"Excuse me," I say politely. "I need to get a drink of water or other reasonable action."

I bolt out of the room. Inside the nearest bathroom, I reassess my strategy. I do not have a Plan B. Unless Plan B is: hide in the bathroom.

I trudge back to the music room.

"Hey, N," Cooper says. "I got Logan and Jessa caught up to speed on your new songs. Here, I've made copies of the algebra lyrics for each of you."

He hands me my printout. And a bottle of water.

"I added a title," Cooper says. "I took it from your lyrics."

I notice the title: "Get Your Algebra On!"

"Um, okay," I say. Whatever. As long as I do not have to party. I sneak a peek at the girl who should be called Jezebel. Jessabel. Jessa—

She's looking back at me! Avert eyes! Retreat! Retreat!

"I thought today we'd work on this one song," Cooper says. "But I did come up with ideas for the others. Like doing the geometry one as heavy metal: 'You've got no proof'—head bang—'if you ain't got a proof'—head bang—'Sucka!'"

I wince but remain silent.

"And chemistry will be a ballad, of course," Cooper

continues. "A romantic lo-o-ove song based on chemistry? The chicks will dig it."

"Do I have to sing any of this?" Logan speaks up. "I can't pronounce half these words."

"No worries, Logan," Jessa reassures him. "I'll be singing the lyrics; you guys can back me up on whatever parts you want. I've taken most of these classes already, so the vocabulary and the concepts are doable for me."

"Jessa's in our school's Accelerated Program," Cooper tells Logan. "Beauty *and* brains."

"Thank you, Cooper," Jessa says. "Now back to business, please. Logan, you're actually very lucky. By the time you get to ninth and tenth grades, you'll have a head start on math and science."

Logan's still in middle school? I didn't know that.

"Eleventh grade too," Cooper says. "I've got Nat's trig/precalc down as a slower rock song and calculus as punk. Physics, I'm not sure yet. Maybe pure pop."

"You did this all while I ate lunch?" I couldn't help saying. Cooper is normally, well, lazy.

"Dude, I know." Cooper shrugs. "I got inspired."

"I'm inspired too!" Jessa says. Even Logan looks less droopy than usual.

Cooper plays the melody he'd been working on. It fits the algebra song quite well. We listen a couple more times to let it sink in.

"Now it's time to party algebra-style!" Cooper riffs on his guitar.

We practice his tune and my lyrics, making adjustments and working together easily. In the midst of the music, I forget everything else that's going on and just play.

Three hours and twelve minutes later we agree we've got it.

"The perfect party song!" Cooper shouts. "All math haters, clear the dance floor!"

"Woohoo!" "Great job!" "Awesome!" Cooper and Jessa and Logan are acting all happy and enthusiastic. They look at me.

"Excuse me," I mumble. "I need to go get a drink of water."

"The mini-fridge is stocked." Cooper points to it just a few feet away from me. There it is. A mini-fridge.

"I—I've got to go," I stammer. I cover my keyboard, grab my papers, and ask where my laptop is.

Cooper says he'll get it. Logan's packing up his stuff. I want to flee.

"Nathaniel," Jessa says. "Are you going to be okay? I'm sorry about the other night, but you have nothing to feel bad about."

"Your mom's left rear tire could use a little more air," I inform her.

"Wha—? Okay, I'll tell her." Awkward silence. "Nathaniel, did I do something wrong?"

Clannnggg . . . Logan's knocked over a cymbal.

"Sorry," he says, lifting it back up. "I'll see you guys tomorrow, right?"

"Yes, see you tomorrow, Logan," Jessa says.

I say good-bye politely. I do not look at Jessa. I do not feel any feelings about Jessa. I am a robot, I am Spock, I am . . . out of here.

I grab my laptop the second Cooper returns with it and escape, without even saying good-bye. I mentally rip up the Be Polite memory card and run back to my house, leaving a trail of imaginary social skills behind me.

CHAPTER SEVENTEEN
CHILL ZONE

Plan C: Clark's Principle of Exclusion (unpublished).

We've been practicing the song "Get Your Algebra On!" for the second day in a row. Today I am implementing Plan C. I have set up a mental firewall against the [Jessa] virus. [ ] = invisible, impenetrable barrier for extra protection.

I have used this tactic over the years against bullies and overly friendly dogs, with mixed success. Thus, it is still a principle and not a law.

"I believe we are ready to film," Cooper announces.

"Now?" [Jessa] squeaks. [She] grabs her bag and runs out of the room.

"Girls." Cooper groans. "Always need to prettify." Then he takes a little bottle of hair gel out of his pocket and applies some to his hair.

Logan and I do not self-improve.

"Now that we're going viral," Cooper says, "we should probably change our name. We don't want to get sued by the company that makes Sprees candy."

I secretly do not think anyone will notice or care. But still. Copyright infringement is serious.

"I think you're right, Cooper," I say, although this means more time spent arguing about a name. *Maybe I can come up with one fast.*

Cooper's tuning his guitar. That gives me an idea.

"How about 'String Theory'?" I say.

"What?" Cooper doesn't look up from his plucking.

"The name for our band?" I repeat. "String Theory?"

"I don't get it," Cooper says.

"How do you spell 'theory'?" Logan asks, *tap-tapping* on his foot pedal.

Fine. I won't even suggest Quantum Loop then. Ignorant teenagers, not even aware of the current controversies in theoretical physics.

"I'm ready." [Jessa] twirls into the room.

"Nice dance moves," Cooper says, "but we're not doing ballet here."

I am glad *he* said it, because pirouettes really would not work with our song and because I cannot speak to [her] myself.

"Oh darn," [Jessa] says. "Two years of dance class down the drain."

"Okay, everyone get into position," Cooper says. "My webcam is set up for a group shot. We'll run through the song once or twice for that. Then I'll use my hand-held camera to take individual close-ups while we play it again. Then one of you guys can film me. This weekend I'll edit it, add some special effects, and send it to each of you for approval Sunday night. By Monday morning, it'll be up on YouTube."

"Cooper Owens, videographer," I say. "Wow."

"Yeah, who knew I was such a tech geek?" Cooper laughs.

"Maybe that can be your major in college," [Jessa] says. "You told me your dad's all over you to choose a summer enrichment camp. You could go to multimedia camp, and that'll look good on your college res, and then you might major in film tech and make it your career!"

"Whoa, whoa, slow down," Cooper says. "[Jess], you're way too ambitious for me. I like to live in the moment. Chill. Be in the zone."

"And what does that mean exactly?" [Jessa] sighs. "You have so much potential, but you want to just *chill* in a *zone*?"

"Actually," I can't stop myself from interrupting,

"a 'chill zone' is a fine-grained border zone in igneous rocks where the melt has cooled by exposure to air or water. It is a geology term."

"How do you *know* this stuff?" Logan says from behind his drum set.

"Two summers ago, I read a book on roadside geology on a family trip to the Adirondack Mountains," I tell him. "The topography there is incredibly intricate."

"Oh, okay." Logan does a little *ba-dum-BAH* and throws his sticks up in the air and catches them on their descent.

"Nice." [Jessa] smiles at him.

"So you compliment Logan for catching sticks . . . but you dis *me* about not having my future planned out?" Cooper mutters. "Not that I'm an expert drumstick catcher, either."

"Cooper, I'm sorry," [Jessa] says. "I know you get enough pressure from your father."

He does?

"I just thought," [she] goes on, "if you gave him an alternative—like multimedia camp—he wouldn't make you go to that military summer program."

What military summer program? Where does [Jessa] get all her information? Do the two of them talk all personal with each other behind our backs? DO

I HAVE TO WORRY ABOUT RULE NUMBER 16 WITH MY BEST FRIEND, TOO???

"Oh," says Cooper. "Huh. Good point. I guess if he's going to force me out of my chill zone, it might as well be to do something cool."

"I think the military is cool," Logan says. "My brother's in the army, and I'm gonna enlist when I turn eighteen."

We're all quiet for twenty-one seconds.

"Okay," Cooper says to Logan. "You'll serve our country while I support you from here in my chill zone."

"You can't be in the chill zone, Cooper," I say. "You're standing on cement, not igneous rock."

Seventeen seconds of quiet.

"You know what?" Cooper says. "I think we should *all* be in the chill zone. As in 'Everybody, let's hear it for the Greatest! Hottest! Band . . . Igneous Rock!'"

"Awesome name," Logan says. "What do you think, Nathaniel?"

"I think it's an oxymoron to say the *hottest* band is *chill*," I mutter.

"Nathaniel?" Cooper stares at me. I bug out my eyes and stare back. I blink first.

"Fine, superduper," I say. "Igneous Rock. Yippee."

"I like it too," [Jessa] says.

"How do you spell 'igneous'?" asks Logan. I tell him. He says it sounds good to him.

"That's settled then." Cooper nods and picks up his guitar. "Who's ready to rock 'n' roll?"

"Rock and roll!" Logan screams in a voice at least forty decibels louder than I've ever heard him.

"ROCK!" Cooper yells.

"And ROLL!" Logan shrieks.

This. Must. Stop.

"Rock!" shouts Cooper.

"Paper, scissors, Spock!" I yell.

"Spock?" Cooper says, and everyone turns to look at me.

I look down at my keyboard, and I play a few notes of a classic TV show theme song: "Star Trek."

"Rock, paper, scissors modified *Star Trek* version," I say. Then I hold up my hand in the universally known Vulcan position. "Live long and prosper."

Cooper, Logan, and even [Jessa] break out laughing. Drat. I wasn't trying to be funny; I was just trying to get the shouting to stop.

Well, at least it worked.

Cooper gets his videocamera ready, and we play the algebra tune over and over. The filming goes really well. We really do have a good band and a good song.

"That's a wrap," Cooper says after one hour and forty-three minutes.

Everyone claps, so I do too.

"I gotta get home," Logan says. "Major essay due tomorrow."

"Yes, I too must go home for . . . "—I need an excuse—"a special program I need to watch." I congratulate myself on successfully completing my [Exclusion] Mission. Barrier dissolve, turn off firewall.

"Nathaniel, wait," Jessa says. "I'll walk over with you. My mom is at your house visiting your mom."

Plan fail. Fail. Fail.

I walk. Jessa speeds up to walk beside me.

"Nathaniel, what's going on?" Jessa says. "Did I do something wrong?"

"Yes," I say, not slowing down my pace.

"What?" she asks. "If I did something that upset you, I'm sorry. I didn't mean to. But it's hard for me to apologize when I don't know what I've done."

You know what you've done, I think. She's a liar, and now she's trying to manipulate me. I am not sure how exactly, but I simply cannot trust Jessa anymore.

We're almost at my front porch.

"Nathaniel." Jessa tugs at my sleeve, dragging me to a stop. She stands next to me, looking up. She lets go of my arm, but I don't move.

"Check out the sky," she says. The setting sun has made the sky various shades of purple and pink. I can see a few stars and Venus, which looks like an especially bright star.

"It's so pretty," Jessa says quietly.

I stand there, face tilted up.

"Did you know," I say, "that there are four galaxies beyond our Milky Way that share the same initials as mine? There's NGC 6822, which is an irregular type one point six million light-years away; NGC 147, elliptical type two point six million light-years away; NGC 185 and NGC 205—same type and distance as 147." I wait. Silence.

"NGC—Nathaniel Gideon Clark. Get it?" I elaborate.

Jessa walks up the steps of my porch and lets herself into my house. The door closes behind her. *I guess she didn't get it.*

I stare up at the sky, thinking about the different NGC galaxies. Finally I go inside and head straight for my room to go online. There's a great intergalactic chat forum on Friday nights.

As they say, TGF! Thank the galaxies it's Friday!

CHAPTER EIGHTEEN
KNOCK 'EM DOWN

My first thought when I wake up?

OSIS! Oh shoot, it's Saturday!

While one would logically conclude I should have been prepared, as Saturday inevitably follows Friday, the day smacks me in the face like a virtual applied force F. ($F = P \times A$, where P is pressure and A is the area over which the force acts, e.g., my face.)

Bowling with Molly. Weekend with Father and his family.

Ergh. . . . I fling my covers over my head and decide to tell my mother I have a headache (caused by $F = P \times A$?).

Zzzzzzzzz.

"Time to wake up, Nathaniel." My mother is in my room.

"Mmmmmrf."

"Are you feeling okay?" Mom has just given me the perfect opportunity to say I don't feel well.

But, in true Aspie form, I cannot tell a lie.

"I'm fine." I crawl out of bed. The headache disappeared while I dozed off.

"Good," Mom says, raising my window blinds. "Molly will be happy to see you."

"Sometimes I wonder." I yawn. "I might just be a person who keeps her from bowling alone. Now, if I had four legs and a mane, it might be different."

"Hmm," Mom hmms. "It's not always easy to understand someone with Asperger's, is it?"

I am not falling into her trap.

"Not according to the diagnostic criteria," I say in a tone equivalent to duh. "I've got to get ready for bowling. Do I really have to go to Dad's?"

"Legally, yes, you do," my mother says. "I'll go fix your breakfast while you get ready."

I get ready and eat breakfast, and then we drive to the bowling alley. All the while I am making up and solving math problems. And quizzing my mother occasionally.

"What is the number of combinations that a committee of three can choose from a group of fifteen people?"

"Twelve," my mom says, braking for a red light.

"You always say 'twelve.'" I dismiss her first answer. "Red light challenge! I'll even give you a hint. It's fifteen factorial divided by three factorial times parenthesis fifteen minus three parentheses factorial."

"Twelve point five," Mom says. The light turns green.

"*Bzzz*, sorry you have lost the red light challenge," I say in a game-show-host voice. "The correct answer is four hundred fifty-five."

"Ooh, I was going to say that next." Mom smacks the steering wheel.

"Mom, you attempted to answer the number of people with a decimal," I say. "Twelve point five people?"

"Oh, we're here already?" Mom pulls into the bowling-alley parking lot. "Darn, I was looking forward to more math interrogation. Well, good-bye, honey. Good luck too. Love you."

"Love you too." I drag my duffel bag and laptop case out of the car and walk to the entrance. I groan under the weight. I despise carrying heavy loads. At least the alley has automatic doors. I go through and drop off my stuff behind the counter. RaShawn, the manager, moves my stuff into his office for safekeeping, hands me my size twelve shoes, and says the same thing he says every week.

"Knock 'em down, kid."

That's why I like it here. It's consistent. I know what to expect.

"Surprise!" Molly jumps up next to me.

Not expected.

"Wha— Oh! Hi," I say.

RaShawn calmly hands Molly size seven shoes and says, "Knock 'em down, kiddo."

We thank RaShawn and head over to our lane, twenty-two, where our balls are waiting as usual. RaShawn takes care of us. I should thank him for that.

"What's up?" I say to Molly.

"I already told you, silly," Molly says, skipping to the lane bench. She opens a bag that is lying there. "A surprise!"

Molly pulls out a white T-shirt with a picture of a light blue bowling ball on it. The holes on the ball are made to look like eyes and a mouth, and there are red squiggly shapes above the holes. I read the words above the picture: Bowling Brainiac.

"I made it for you," Molly says, grinning. "With fabric paint and iron-on letters. See the brains up there? Do you like it?"

"I do like it," I tell her. "I'm going to wear it now." I pull the T-shirt over my long-sleeved henley shirt.

Molly laughs as I show off my new look.

"What is the occasion?" I want to know.

"It's our meet-i-versary!" Molly says. "We met exactly five years ago today!"

It occurs to me that Molly is a very good friend and that I *am* more than just a bowling buddy.

"This is great," I say. "You're a good friend."

"I know," Molly says. "Look, I made one for myself, too." She takes a pink shirt out of the bag and holds it up. It also has a bowling ball face, but instead of squiggles, it has . . . "A mane!" Molly points out. It says: Bowling Mane-iac.

"Put it on, Molly Mane-iac," I encourage her, and she layers it on over her shirt. Perhaps we look like a couple of dorks with matching handmade shirts, but who cares?

We are who we are.

Molly and I bowl our two games. My scores are 122 and 148, Molly's are 68 and . . . 101!

"I did it!" Molly shrieks. "Over one hundred!"

"Triple digits," I say, giving her a high five.

We switch back into our regular foot attire.

"Alex invited me to a party," Molly says. "It's his next-door neighbor's birthday, and we're going with his parents, so of course I'm nervous; but I have a new dress, and I'm going to get my ears pierced after school on Tuesday."

"Wow," I say. It is an all-purpose "wow." I am not actually *wowed*.

"It's a pretty big party," Molly goes on. "So it will be crowded and loud, but Alex says we can leave early it if gets to be too much for me. He's thoughtful like that. That's why for my thirteenth birthday I didn't even *want* a party, just an extra day at the stables. I don't like to be around a lot of people, but a lot of horses is totally different."

"Wait." I let my mind catch up with her words. "Did you say thirteenth birthday party? Like a Bat Mitzvah?"

"Yup," Molly says. "His neighbor's Jewish, so Alex will have to wear a kippah—a little hat—for the actual ceremony, but not at the party afterward. That's at a banquet hall."

"Guess what?" I say. "I think my band is playing at that party."

"Your band?" Molly frowns. "You have a band?"

"I'm *in* a band," I say, looking at her. "Didn't you know that?"

"How would I know that?" Molly says. "You never told me about it."

Mindblind.

It occurs to me that perhaps I have not been the best friend I could be. I guess I don't really tell Molly much about my life.

"Yeah, I play keyboard, and we have our own practice room in my friend Cooper's garage," I say. "We're actually pretty good."

"I was going to be in band in fourth grade, but every time I practiced my flute, our dog, Bradley, would howl," Molly says, talking really fast. "And I didn't like all the mistakes the other flute kids in my row made. It made me want to scream. Actually, one day I *did* scream, and the band teacher and my parents agreed to switch me to the resource room during that hour."

Okay, maybe it wasn't totally my fault that Molly did not know things about me. She does not give me much opportunity to say anything.

"My father's here," I say. "Gotta go." We stand up.

"'Bye," Molly says, turning left to get her usual snack at the vending machines. I turn right toward the entryway.

I slowly walk up to the counter to return my shoes. I pay for the games.

"Thank you," I say to RaShawn. "For everything."

"Sure, kid," he says, and then starts ringing out a group of women wearing red hats. I wonder if they take off their hats for bowling or if it is some kind of cult that requires them to keep on their hats at all times. Like burkas. (I am avoiding facing my father. Who is right here.)

"Ready, Nathaniel?" my father asks.

I. Feel. Queasy. No more stalling. My father walks out through the automatic doors, and I follow him.

Potentially to my Doom. I had gotten drunk, made a scene, and thrown up in my father's best client's kitchen. My father has gone ballistic on me for far less than this.

CHAPTER NINETEEN
CRIME AND PUNISHMENT

I am in the passenger seat. My father is in the driver's seat. We are both looking straight ahead. Our gazes extended would never meet on a coordinate plane. Parallel, with no point of intersection.

"I have been getting quite an earful from both your mother and your stepmother," says my father. "Just one of them on my case is enough, but two women? Phew. I've taken quite a beating."

What do I say to that? I choose nothing.

"I went to a counselor on Wednesday," my father says, merging onto the highway. "I admit, I did not want to go, but Rachel and Andrea and your Dr. Ali insisted."

I notice the acceleration lane is longer than normal. Must be because of the uphill grade. That's good engineering.

My father picks up something out of the cup holder and holds it out to me.

"The counselor wrote this down and said to give it to you," he says. It is a piece of paper. I am curious. I read it.

From the desk of Mary Jeanne Robinson, MSW, LCSW

Nathaniel, here is a puzzle. Can you decipher it? I'll give you a hint—the theme is "family."

—MJR

$$f_i + s_i = 0 \text{ and } F_{ST} + S_N = f_i + s_i$$

I love puzzles. How did she know?

"Ms. Robinson has a son, Jake, who is your age. She says he has Asperger's syndrome," my father says, "which is why Rachel chose her. Ms. Robinson asked me what you were interested in, and I said math. She said her son draws."

"You don't believe in Asperger's syndrome," I remind him. "You say it's just an excuse for me being spoiled or immature."

"Exactly." My father gives a little cough. "I don't believe in labeling your behavior as a 'syndrome.' But the counselor and I agreed to disagree for now."

He refuses to listen, to even try.

I feel the rage growing in me as if it were a tangible thing. I want to yell and hit and curse and destroy....

$$f_i + s_i = 0 \text{ and } F_{ST} + S_N = f_i + s_i$$

I want to figure this out. The formula has distracted me.

"It has to do with family," I think out loud so my father will not keep talking and interfere with my concentration. Or say something else to tick me off.

"The lowercase f could stand for 'father,' which might make the s a 'son.' Or f could be 'family' and s a 'system.' . . . No, that makes no sense. It appears to be 'father' and 'son.'

"*Sub i* makes them imaginary. An imaginary father plus an imaginary son equals zero."

I close my eyes and observe as the remaining symbols and images rearrange themselves.

My eyes snap open. I've got it.

"F is capitalized, which makes it a specific father. In this case, F *sub ST* means 'Steven.' That's you. And the specific son S *sub N* is me: 'Nathaniel.'"

There. Solved.

"So, what exactly does that mean?" My father sighs.

Sheesh, I thought it was obvious. I do not want to speak to my father, but my need to show off is overpowering.

"Basically," I say in what is known as my I'm superior-to-you tone of voice that gets me in a lot of trouble so I use it less often than I used to. Unless I forget. Which is still often. "Basically it says that when there is simply an *idea* of a father and son, the relationship is imaginary. It equals zero. It means nothing. But," I say, darting a glance at my father to see if he is listening.

"But . . . ?" he says. It appears he is listening, so I continue.

"But in the specific Steven-Nathaniel equation, their sum cannot equal zero. Together, they have to add up to *something*. Something real, not imaginary."

"You got all that from that little paper?" my father says. He takes exit 17E and stops at a red light at the end of the exit. "Ms. Robinson also said it might take you a few days to figure out that puzzle and that you could e-mail her if you had questions."

"It took me forty-seven seconds," I say. "And I don't have questions. It is perfectly clear."

The light turns green; my father turns left. Five more minutes to my father's house.

What my mother and Dr. Ali have told me is that my father expects me to fit into an idea he has of how his son *should* be in order to maintain his self-image.

"The puzzle says you are leaving me out of the equation," I say bravely. My father turns onto his street.

My father does not respond to my bravery. He says nothing.

We're almost at the driveway. I want out of this car! This is a waste of time. Since when do I get my hopes up? Since when do I want him to try to meet my needs? Besides, what do I *need* from him? I need NOTHING from him. I need him to leave me alone.

Open File: C:\My Files\Nightmare.avi (Date 10/2/98)
"Daddy!" I wake up crying. I've had a nightmare and I need my daddy. He's strong and brave and scares the night demons away.
Close File.

Up the driveway, into the three-car garage, we stop next to Rachel's Volvo.

"Ms. Robinson said you could contact her about anything else you want to know," my father says. "Her e-mail address is on the back of that paper."

He unbuckles, gets out of the vehicle, and goes into the house. Finally. Peace and quiet. I stay in the passenger seat and flip over the paper.

E-mail: mjrobinson@sw.com is written in the same black pen and handwriting as the puzzle. But I notice something else. At the very bottom, in the right-hand corner, something is lightly penciled in:

KICK ASP!

Kick Asp. In funky letters. That's funny. Funny-strange and funny-ha-ha. Then I remember that the counselor has a son with Asperger's. Maybe he doodled it. I do not doodle. Another example of how not all Aspies are alike.

I grab my weekend bags, stuffing the paper into an outside pocket, fumble with the car-door handle, and get out. Then my duffel bag strap gets caught on a small bike. The bike crashes sideways into the car; and I pitch forward, tripping on my own feet, and land *splat* on the garage floor.

I remain there for a moment, not wanting to get up. When I realize why, I get up quickly, put the bicycle upright, and check the car for damages. Not even a scratch. Big *Whew*.

I drag myself and my stuff out of the garage and into my father's mudroom. I've narrowly escaped punishment for scratching car or breaking bike, but I know there is far, far worse to come. I have yet to be bawled out for the drinking–puking–Dad's client's–house party situation.

"Na-thaniel!"

Joshua Paul Clark shouts gleefully and wraps himself around my leg. Which brings me, and my bags, down on the floor again.

"Body slam!" Joshua jumps up and dances around. "I'm getting big. I weigh thirty-eight libs and two ozzes. Daddy's scale told me."

Although I'm disgruntled by having to pull myself up off the floor *again*, I also can't help being amused.

"Well, I weigh one hundred thirty-five libs and zero ozzes," I say.

"But I have muscles." Joshua pushes up his sleeve and flexes his arm. I almost tell him *everybody* has muscles, when I realize what he means.

"You are a tough guy, all right," I say.

I let him give me a bear hug and squeeze as hard as he can to prove it.

Joshua skips out of the kitchen singing "I'm a TUFF guy" while I recover. That kid is surprisingly strong. I might even have bruises.

My little half brother could probably KICK my ASP.

"Nathaniel!" my father's voice calls out. "Can you come into the family room? Rachel and I want to talk to you."

Oh, crap. (Yes, I cursed. The occasion calls for it.) I am about to face Sir Steven the Strict, the evil paternus, harbinger of doom.

"What if I do not want to hear what you have to say?" I yell back.

There is a pause. I hear Rachel saying something to my father, but I cannot make out the words.

"Nathaniel?" he calls again. "*Please* get in here."

"Coming," I say. I sludge (slow + trudge) across the kitchen, stepping only on the yellow tiles. Except one turns out to be a yellow SpongeBob toy; and when I step on it, it squawks "I'm a goofy goober, yeah! You're a goofy goober, yeah!"

I enter the family room and sit down on a puffy round ottoman. My father and Rachel are together on the couch, looking serious.

The firing squad.

"I sent Joshua upstairs to watch cartoons on the big-screen," Rachel says.

What if they take away my computer? I cannot live without my computer! Oh please, please, just ground me. I love being grounded as it does not affect my life. Just tell me!

I am pacing back and forth, mumbling to myself.

When did I get up off the ottoman? Spaced out there. I go back to the ottoman and face my father and his wife.

"What's my punishment?" I blurt out.

"What? What punishment?" Rachel asks. "Didn't your mother tell you you're not in any trouble?"

Oh. I thought that was just at her house. I assumed

there was no carryover to my father's house. Usually my divorced parents live in a Venn diagram, with only one overlapping item in the middle: me.

"You did nothing wrong," Rachel assures me. "Now other people? They messed up big and are having to deal with the consequences."

She crosses her arms and whistles *doo-dee-doo.*

"I'm waiting," she says.

"Yes, okay, that would be me," my father says. "I'm sorry, Nathaniel. I was wrong to make you go to that party." He says it in a way that makes me wonder if he is being sincere. It's just a feeling; I cannot really tell.

"Duh," I say, very very quietly. Under my breath. *No freaking DUH.*

"Although what's wrong with trying to get your son out of the house and being social?" my father continues, negating his apology.

"Nathaniel, there is something else we need to tell you." Rachel interrupts him.

RED FLAG! ALERT!

Open Red-flagged File: C:\My Files\baby1.avi (Date 2/16/06)
"Nathaniel, there is something we need to tell you," my father says, taking New Wife's hand.

"You're going to be a big brother!" Rachel exclaims.

Uh. "Okay," I say. I leave the room and head up the stairs. I have one hundred pages of Dostoyevsky's *Crime and Punishment* to get through this weekend. Required reading for World Lit credits. Usually, I think of fiction as a waste of time, but not when it gets me my diploma. Fortunately, I am a speed-reader.

"Nathaniel!" My father comes after me and catches up with me in the hallway. "That was extremely rude. Rachel says we're having a baby, and you just disappear?"

I check. I have not disappeared. I am still visible, but in some sort of trouble.

"The appropriate response would be 'Congratulations!'" my father says. "It's an exciting, happy thing to bring new life into this world!"

"A new life is brought into this world every eleven seconds," I say. "The results of human procreation are an extremely common event."

"*Aaah!*" The sound emanating from my father is unpleasant. "Nathaniel?" he says.

"What?"

"Next time someone gives you good news, just say 'Congratulations.'"

"Okay." I shrug. "I did not realize it was good news. Congratulations." I go into my room and shut my door on the inevitable confusion of interacting with my father.

Close File.

"Congratulations!" I say heartily. "Congratulations

on your good news!"

My father and Rachel have funny looks on their faces. "Congratulations on what good news?" my father says.

"You're having a baby." Do I have to spell it out for them? *B-A-B-Y*.

Rachel snorts. I'm a little impressed. She is not the snorting type, and that was a good one.

"I'm not pregnant," she tells me. "No more babies. But thank you, anyway. You were very polite, if completely off base."

"Let's get back on track here," my father says. "We have something *else* to tell you. It's about . . ."

"'THANIEL!" Joshua hollers from upstairs. "Help! I *need* you!"

"For what?" my father yells back.

"I made poop in the potty!" Joshua replies.

For an instant my eyes meet my father's, and there is a distinct possibility we are thinking the same thing.

"Joshie, I'm coming up to help," Rachel calls.

"But I want Na-thaniel," Joshua says in a whiny voice.

Rachel looks at me and says "Sit" and goes off to the upstairs level.

Um.

Uck. Yuck.

Uh.

"How 'bout we get something to eat?" My father jumps up from the couch.

"Yes!" I say, hopping up just as quickly. I would much rather go to my room, but I am extremely hungry. I am not allowed to eat up there when my father is around due to him believing I am a slob when I eat.

I grab a bag of pretzels and a box of fish crackers from the cupboard. My father grabs a bottle of lemonade and a bottle of Miller Lite beer from the fridge. We head back into the family room. My father sits down on the couch and clicks on the TV. I lie down on the floor on my stomach, the snacks and beverages on a table within reach.

There is automobile racing on. NASCAR. I usually do not watch this type of program. Dr. Ali has suggested in the past that I try to find something that my father and I both can enjoy together without much talking/ arguing. I would not have guessed NASCAR; but as I munch the snacks, I find myself relaxing. Numbers and times and placements and lap counts run across the top of the screen as the cars zoom around.

I do some race-related combinatorics and probabilities in my head for fun.

There are just twelve laps to go, with a driver named

Kurt Busch in the lead, when I fall asleep.

I am dreaming.

I'm buckled into the passenger seat of a Miller Lite–sponsored race car. I look over and see that Kurt Busch is driving. I only see his helmet, not his face, but Dream Me knows it is him.

We are zooming into the final lap when The Miller Lite car blows by us.

Kurt Busch shrugs.

"You can't win 'em all," he says.

Suddenly I am out of the car, standing in a crowd of people cheering for the first-place driver, who stands in the winner's circle. With Jessa. Jessa gives him a kiss, and the crowd cheers more.

The winner waves his flaps in the air. *His flaps???* I see that he is a Pokemon creature: Shroomish (Lv. 11 HP 60). The mushroom Pokemon.

"Nathaniel!" it calls out to me. "Hey, don't you re-member who I am? Don't you like green eggs and ham, Sam-I-Am?"

Sam-I-Am?

Then the Shroomish spouts poison stun spores from the top of his head. They hit me, and I am para-lyzed! I try to muster my own Poke-power. But my legs won't work. I need backup. I need help.

CHAPTER TWENTY
ZOOM IN

Open File: C:\My Files\BradenParty_Jessa.avi (Date 10/12/10)

"You take one arm," Cooper is saying, "I'll take the other." My arms are draped over the shoulders of Cooper and . . . Jessa's boyfriend. They are half carrying, half dragging me out of the house onto the front lawn.

I do not want to see this. But the movie plays on.

"Nathaniel, you'll be okay," I hear Jessa say. Is she crying? She sounds as if she's crying.

"Hey, by the way, dude," Cooper says, "I'm Cooper, Nathaniel's best friend."

"Oh, okay," he says. "I'm Sam, Jessa's cousin."

PAUSE. UNPAUSE.

"I just moved here from Kansas City," Sam says.

"Sam and Jade and Nathaniel and I used to play together

when he came to visit." Jessa sniffles.

PAUSE. ZOOM IN.

I take a closer look at Sam's face. That's Jessa's cousin Sam? He got so much older! Last time I saw him we were ten. And short. And we both liked Pokemon. Loved Pokemon. Played, talked, and obsessed—together.

UNPAUSE.

"Yeah, Nathaniel was awesome," Sam says. "Those were good times."

"There's his father's car," Cooper says.

"Thank God," says Jessa. "Nathaniel, everything is going to be okay."

Close File.

I wake up fast. Holy crud. That was the file the avatar gave me. The one I wouldn't look at. The memory I'd buried during my drunk blackout.

It hits me. *Sam.* That was Sam?

That was Sam! Jessa's cousin, my old friend! He is not her boyfriend! She did not break rule number sixteen. She did not break anything.

The Jessa I'd thought I knew was real. Oops. I have some serious apologizing to do. I am not a good apologizer, but I will have to come up with something.

Strangely, I don't feel bad or embarrassed or overwhelmed thinking about the party anymore. ("Delete!"

my avatar had said.) I just feel as if I need to fix the misunderstanding so Jessa and I can move on with our lives.

It was just one bad party. It was just one bad evening. It was just life.

I cannot fix things while I am still on the floor. I need to get moving.

My father is still on the couch, with a mostly empty bottle of beer in his hand. The television now shows a ball sports game with the score of 17 to 3.

I get up, still a bit disoriented, and go to the guest bathroom. Yech. My reflection in the mirror shows that the left half of my face is textured like the carpet. And a piece of my hair is sticking straight up (but that's normal). I rub my face with a damp washcloth, which wakes me up and smooths my face, and return to the family room.

"I'm going up to my room," I tell my father. I cannot wait to e-mail Jessa.

"Not yet," my father says.

Not yet? Unexpected! He is always glad to get rid of me.

"I need to tell you a few things," says my father. "Sit."

I sigh. I sit. It takes a lot of willpower for me not to continue my plan to go straight upstairs. But I choose to be flexible. Okay, I choose not to be yelled at.

Summary:

1. Braden's father and stepmother have been arrested for endangering the welfare of a minor, providing alcohol to minors, and two counts of drug possession. They are both currently out on bail but face serious consequences.

2. Braden's mother came in from California and took custody of him. So Braden's now living in Sacramento (far enough away to keep him from trying to get revenge on me and anyone else who wrecked his party and got his father busted).

3. Before I had even drunk the punch, two people at the party called the police to report what was going on.

4. After he dropped me off at home, my father had driven to the police station, where he gave a report against his client. FORMER client. Because even though my father is a jerk, he is not stupid enough to continue "personal coaching" a guy going to jail. And, apparently, Jessa, Cooper, and Sam had asked him to go to the police because an adult would be more credible.

5. It was a one-sided conversation, with my father doing all of the talking. An expression came into my mind that I never would have thought would apply to me:

Dumbstruck.

Struck dumb. (Dumb in this instance means "mute, not speaking" and is not a description of my intelligence.)

Dumbstruck.

"You went to the police because my friends asked you to?" I ask, finally retrieving my voice.

"Well," my father says, "it also looks good for business: Steven Clark helps put away the bad guys. Personal empowerment and citizen safety!"

Oh yeah. Justice has been served. My dad, the hero (sarcasm). I do not know what to say.

"May I go upstairs now?"

"Yes," my father replies, and turns back to his game.

"You're lucky you were down there," Rachel says as we meet on the stairs. "It was an ugly scene. Everything is all cleaned up now, and Josh had a bath."

I'm on the computer seven minutes later when I hear a small knock. "Come in," I say. Why not? I'm just playing Tetris, so I guess I can deal with company. I turn and watch as the door cracks open; a little face peeks through.

"I'm clean," Joshua says.

"I heard," I say. "Want to play LEGO Star Wars with me?"

"Yeah!" Joshua shouts, racing over and leaping onto

my bed, where I am set up with the laptop. He moves in close so we can both see the screen.

Joshua's hair is damp, and he smells like a mixture of Mr. Bubble, mint toothpaste, and chocolate.

The chemistry of a small boy who happens to share my father—and my father's genes—with me. I wonder what that combination does for my scent.

"What do I smell like?" I ask Joshua.

He makes an exaggerated sniff.

"Like a brother," he says, leaning into me.

He may be my brother, but he shows no mercy on the Planet Tatooine. Within three minutes my player has been decapitated.

Joshua cheers as my character breaks into pieces and the body parts fall to the ground.

CHAPTER TWENTY-ONE
THAWING THE CHILL

I wake up on Sunday afternoon after a superlong marathon sleep. I want to get to my e-mail, but my body has other ideas. My stomach is growling loudly. It needs food. When I go downstairs, I am greeted by Rachel and Joshua.

"He's awake!" Joshua smiles. "No more 'Shh . . . sh . . . *quiet* voice,' right, Mommy?"

"Right," Rachel says. "Good sleep, Nathaniel?"

No dreams. No nightmares. No interruptions.

"Yes," I say.

"You must be starving," Rachel says. "I'll warm up the pasta and toast some garlic bread for you. Sound good?"

"Yes," I say. "Thank you for being so thoughtful."

"Mommy's not a wicked stepmother," Joshua informs

me. "She's my mommy and your stepmother." He starts walking around the kitchen saying "Step, step, step . . . mother."

"Oh, okay," I say.

"And we don't have no dungeon either," he adds. "I go build one! You can come see it, Nathaniel. Don't worry. I won't put you in it. Only the bad guys! And pirates!" And he runs off.

Joshua is supposed to be the normal child, but I still do not understand why.

Mmmm . . . pasta. I spend the next forty-three minutes carbo-loading. Rachel has even made chocolate brownies for dessert. I am satiated. Now I have things to do.

"Oh, Dr. Ali called," Rachel says. "He'd like you to call him back."

Now I have more things to do.

Wash hands. Call Dr. Ali's service. Wait. He calls back and asks how I am. I tell him about my retrieved memory and watching NASCAR with my father. At first I am embarrassed (it's *NASCAR!*), but Dr. Ali says that sounds good. He says I'm doing a good job processing things and that my mother should call the office tomorrow to set up an appointment for later this week.

I am about to say good-bye when I hear strange squeaking and chattering. Is it our connection? Is something wrong with the phone?

I ask.

"No, no," Dr. Ali says. "It's my daughter's electronic hamsters. They're racing around all over the floor, and I do not know how to stop them."

"You have a daughter?" I ask.

"Three daughters," Dr. Ali says. "And at least one of them had better come here RIGHT NOW and turn off these rodents!"

"Um, good-bye then?" I say.

"Nathaniel, good-bye," Dr. Ali says. And before he clicks off I hear him yell "Girls! Now!" and more squeaky noises.

It occurs to me that I have not given much thought to Dr. Ali's life outside of his office.

It also occurs to me that I really do not need to. I have *other* people to think about today. I go upstairs and carefully craft an e-mail.

Jessa, I am sorry about how I treated you. It was a misunderstanding. I hope you can forgive me. If you cannot, I still want to play in the band and hope you do too.

Sincerely, Nathaniel

P.S. Do you think Sam would be ok if you gave me his e-mail? Your cousin Sam from Kansas City?

<Send>

Next I scroll down through my unread mail, deleting most of it. Then I open the most recent one. It is from Cooper, who sent the message just twenty minutes ago.

NGC! Check this out . . . Coop

There is a link to YouTube, so I click on it.

"An Igneous Rock Production."

The words *Igneous* and *Rock* are slabs of minerals. There is a cartoon volcano to the right of the text.

Suddenly the volcano erupts, spewing lava onto *Igneous* and *Rock*; and all of the letters begin melting, dripping down the screen. I hear . . . Cooper's guitar!

And there we are, the four of us, with the text "Get Your Algebra On!" in the lower left-hand corner.

Jessa starts singing. She sounds amazing and looks amazing. Logan's red hair is flying, and his drumsticks blur, he's drumming so hard; and Cooper looks cool, as usual, on his expensive guitar; . . . and there is me.

I did not know I looked like that.

I mean, I check myself in the mirror every day, but I don't really *look* at myself. It's just— *There's my hair, face is clean, shirt's on right side out (a long-term*

*issue for me), pants aren't too nerdily pulled up—
okay, I'm done.*

But here on the screen is a different person.

A tall, blond guy on the keyboard who is rocking
out. No technical musical errors, of course; but it's
more than watching a decent musician.

I could be mistaken, but I think I look cool.
Confident. Video Me looks as if he is having a good
time.

The shot cuts to Jessa's face (*she looks beautiful*),
music plays, there are special effects and close-ups of
each of us, and then it ends with our band fading out
visually and aurally. The word *Chill* appears on the
screen and stays for five seconds.

Then it's over.

Wow. That was really good.

I type a reply to Cooper—

Wow. That was really good.

<Send>

I'm watching it over again when I receive an e-
mail from Cooper. I pause the video and open the
message:

Dude, you really think it's good? C

I reply:

I really think it is great! N

<Send>

I go back to watching our music video. When it is done, I close YouTube and go back to e-mail. Cooper's already responded.

N—Thanx! Logan called and said it was awesome! Jessa texted that it rocks! We rock! C

C—We chill zone igneous Rock! N

<Send>

Nathaniel, Cooper gave me your e-mail address. Dosen't the video look awesome? Sincerly, Logan Finley

Logan, it is awesome! Your drumming is awesome! Best, Nathaniel

<Send>

Nathaniel, that means a lot coming from a genius like u. C Ya. Logan Finley

Ergh. I consider notifying Logan that I, in fact, am not a genius. But I don't have the energy to get into it now. That was a whirlwind of social activity. Except. I did not hear from Jessa. Hmm. Cooper did. Well, maybe she is taking some time to compose her message of forgiveness, to get the words just right. I'll give her some time to respond to me.

A response! Oh, it's just Cooper.

N—We rock igneously in the chill zone! C

Cooper making no sense.

C—That makes no sense. N

<Send>

N—I think we shld shoot the chemistry video next. We'll have to wait til after our Sat gig. 6-8-59.

Oh, that's so funny! I am pleased that Cooper remembers his periodic table of elements name! I translated our names into chem code when we were nine. Each number corresponds to the element on the periodic table, and then you take the first letters or symbol and spell it out. For 6-8-59:

6-Carbon: C

8-Oxygen: O

59-Praseodymium: Pr

COPr. Cooper!

So it isn't exact. That's why it's a code.

I reply using our code names.

6-8-59,

OK!

7. 17-18-19.

<Send>

I grin at my code name: N. Clark. (Nathaniel was too unwieldy and didn't look right in the code.) But N. ClArK (Nitrogen. Chlorine—Argon—Potassium) works great.

"Whatchadoin'?" a small voice says from behind me.

"Aah!" I jump off my swivel chair.

It's Joshua. Joshua has entered my room. I remind

myself for the sixty-third time to ask my father to help me turn my computer desk around so that it faces the door instead of the outside window. Then I can see a person if (s)he happens to come in without knocking. Which (s)he is not supposed to do at any time.

"You are supposed to knock," I inform Joshua.

"I did," he says. "I did too knock."

Oh. I've been known to not hear well when I'm on the computer.

"Well, you startled me coming in behind my back like that," I say, still out of sorts.

"Why don'tchoo use your laptop on the bed?" Joshua says, sticking his fingers in his mouth. "Then no one is behind you."

I look over at my bed. He's right. Why don't I use my laptop on my bed, where I have a view of the entire room, including the door?

Because it hadn't occurred to me. That's why.

"So whatchadoin'?" Joshua says again.

I want to say "Big people stuff you wouldn't understand."

"Come here, I'll show you," I say instead.

Joshua stands next to me, watching as I close the program and start up Word.

"What's your last name?" I ask Joshua.

"Joshua," he says.

"No, your other one."

"Paul."

"After that," I persist.

"Clark," he says.

"You want to see 'Clark' written in a secret code?" I say.

"Want to see Joshua," he says.

Okay. There's no *J* on the periodic table.

"No, really, Clark is cool," I tell him. "Clark is *my* last name too! We share it!"

"We do?" Joshua's eyes go wide. "Cool!"

I type the numbers *17*, *18*, and *19*.

"That's seventeen, eighteen, and nineteen," I tell him. "The top secret chemical code for 'Clark.'" I print him a copy on my wireless printer.

"Thank you," Joshua says very seriously. Then, waving the paper in his hand, he runs out of my room. Through the open door, I hear him yell, "Mommy! Senteen, eighteen, nineteen! That's me and 'Thaniel's top secret code!"

I check my e-mail again. Spam, spam, Boston University Admissions Deadline, spam.

Nothing from Jessa.

I guess I will have to wait a little more. Waiting is not a personal strength of mine, but I am sure it won't be too long. She will respond to me soon.

I'll wait.

Waiting . . . still waiting . . .

CHAPTER TWENTY-TWO

TWO FACES AND PERSONAL SPACES

Back at home. Two full days later. It is Tuesday afternoon. I am still waiting. I am actively working on my "slacking" skills, watching television in the living room. The History Channel is showing a special on the history of weather. Otherwise I'd be watching the Weather Channel. I've always enjoyed meteorology as a minor interest.

Right now they are discussing the origins of the Saffir-Simpson Hurricane Wind Scale. Someday I can be famous for the Nathaniel Clark Scale of . . . hmmm . . . Clark Scale of . . .

Blrrrrpt. I fart.

. . . the Nathaniel Clark Scale of Gas Expulsion Speed.

On a scale of one to rip-roaring ten, that was a nine.

I stretch out on the couch in my raggedy sweats. Something I dislike about peer fashion pressure: Why does wearing sweatpants make you a geek? They are so comfortable, affordable, and easy to pull up and down. But no! In public I must wear jeans with difficult buttons and scratchy fabric interiors.

I slack some more. This does not come naturally to me, slacking and watching TV. When I was younger, my mother forced me to watch PBS Kids and Nickelodeon and Disney Channel. She believed that having knowledge of pop culture would help me relate to my peers. She was correct. I could talk *Bob the Builder* and *Fairly OddParents* and discern the difference between *Blue's Clues*'s Steve and Joe. Zack versus Cody. Even Hannah and Miley.

Not that I wanted to know these things . . . or cared. But my mother added it to the interpersonal social skills part in my school curriculum. So I studied kids' shows. Until I was eleven and a high school graduate. Then my mother took TV watching out of the curriculum, stating that today's teen pop culture is *not* necessary to my moral and social development. Television off.

(Except *The Amazing Race*. That's in a category by itself.)

Yawn. This slackout is a little boring. I am debating what to do next when Jessa walks into the room.

Jessa walks into the room???

I sit up, the slacker me vanishing and leaving just me—in sloppy sweats. (Since when do I feel self-conscious about my clothes? Since when do I feel self-conscious?)

"You could say hi," Jessa says.

I could? I could. "Hi," I say brilliantly.

Jessa stands there.

"Um, what do you want?" I say. Even I realize that sounded wrong. "I mean, what are you doing here?"

"Your e-mail said you were sorry," Jessa says. "You said you wanted me to forgive you for a misunderstanding. Well, I am not ready to forgive you."

It feels as if a rock has dropped in the pit of my stomach. A rock with a very large mass and a high number on Mohs scale of mineral hardness.

"We are supposed to be friends," Jessa continues. "Friends don't freeze each other out when they have a problem. You stopped speaking to me, Nathaniel, and I have no idea why. If I'm going to forgive you, I need to know what I'm forgiving you *for*."

I go blank. Friendship blank. Love blank.

"Did you know," my mouth says, "it is now acceptable to use a preposition at the end of a sentence?"

"Nice," Jessa mutters. "I'll see you at the bat mitzvah on Saturday." She turns and walks out of the room.

Uh-oh.

I must activate my own powers, bringing all of my feelings to the surface and letting them out into the world. For Jessa.

"Wait!" I jump up from the couch and race out of the room. Jessa is at the front door, with her hand on the doorknob.

"Wait," I say again.

A few seconds pass.

"Well?" Jessa says.

"Oh, I was just making sure you were going to wait," I say. I take a deep breath and exhale the fluster out.

"I stopped speaking to you," I say, "because I thought you'd broken rule sixteen."

"Rule sixteen?" says Jessa. Her forehead wrinkles up. "The dating rule?"

"I saw you with a guy at the party and thought you were going behind your parents' back and had a boyfriend and lied to me." The words whoosh out of me.

Jessa takes her hand off the doorknob and turns to face me. Is that a smile? The corners of her mouth are lifting up. That indicates a smile. Why is she happy all of a sudden?

"You thought my cousin Sam was my boyfriend?" asks Jessa. "Sam?"

"Yes, I did not realize who he was until later," I mumble. "Much later."

Jessa makes a sputterylaughingsnorty sound. I don't even attempt to interpret it.

"But you *know* Sam," Jessa says.

"I know ten-year-old Sam," I retort. "He is not exactly the same now. I did not recognize him, okay?"

When I feel foolish, my voice tends to rise and get defensive.

"Sorry." I retreat. "It's just that I thought you were— what do people call it—having two faces?"

"Two-faced," Jessa says. "No, I just have one, boring, boyfriendless face."

"It's not boring," I say. "It's beautiful."

Oh. No. $N = m^{1,000,000,000,000,000}$ where m = mortification.

I don't know what to do. This is unprecedented. I want to run away, but my feet don't listen to my brain. I'm stuck.

$2, 4, 16, 256 \ldots \pi = 3.1415 \ldots$ Racing through my mind is an irrational variety of patterns and numbers.

"Really?" Jessa breaks into my thoughts. "You think I'm beautiful?"

"Well, yes," I respond. I cannot be anything but honest. "And you're smart and fun and talented and smart."

I realize I've said that already and stop there to prevent a verbal loop from forming.

There. That was easy. *Not! (Sarcasm.) I'm sweating like a pig. (Simile.) I'm freaking out. (Slang.) I'm . . .* being spoken to.

"Well," Jessa says. "This is an interesting turn of events."

She steps closer toward me. I believe she has crossed into my culturally established personal space.

"Did you know," Jessa says, her eyes meeting mine and capturing them, "that rule number sixteen covers only dating?"

I can feel her breath. She smells citrusy.

"There is no age restriction on my first kiss," she says.

"Have you—um—had that first kiss?" I ask, not sure what she's getting at; but an idea is starting to form.

"Nope," Jessa says. Then she steps back away from me. "So, I'll see you at the bat mitzvah Sunday?"

Wait? Didn't we just have a "moment"? Wasn't that a "moment"?

I decide it was. And, uncharacteristically, I decide there needs to be another one.

"Jessa," I say, taking hold of her arm and gently spinning her toward me. She's wearing a black fleece that feels like velvet. I take her other arm and step into her space.

Her eyes get wide, but I don't back down. I am focused and determined. I lean down and cup my hand under Jessa's chin.

I stop.

"Is this okay?" I ask. I mean both *"Is this okay with the rules?"* and *"Is this okay with you?"*

Jessa nods up and down. Thank God I know what that nonverbal sign means.

I kiss her. A brief (2.5 seconds) moment of my lips meeting her lips. It's working! The kiss is working! I pull away. *Now what???*

"Was that okay?" I say.

Jessa puts her hand on the back of my neck and pulls me in and gives me another brief, soft kiss.

Wow.

"Better than okay." Jessa smiles. Then she stops smiling and bites her lower lip. "Nathaniel? Will *you* be okay with this? I mean, rule number sixteen still stands. No boyfriends. But I'm really happy we . . . did that."

"So, we're friends that kissed?" I say. "Well, okay. I suppose it's better than being 'kissing cousins.'"

Jessa groans.

"Was that a joke, Nathaniel Clark?" she says. "Are you making a joke at this very important moment?"

"Uh—no—uh—sorry," I stammer.

"I'm kidding!" Jessa says, lightly punching me in the

arm. "It *was* funny, and we *are* friends, and I will always remember my first kiss. With you." And then she's out the door with a "'Bye!'"

I do not know what normal, neurotypical people do after they have successfully engaged in kissing the girl they love.

What I do is go to the refrigerator and take out an orange and carefully slice it into quarters. Then I carry the orange up to my room.

I set my portable DVD player to play "*The Amazing Race* Season One, Episode One." I own the whole season's four-disk set plus commentary and bonus features. Sometimes it is nice to go back and watch the show when it was fresh and new. Right from the beginning.

Beginnings can be terrifying to an Aspie—so much unknown and uncharted. But after it's over, it can be wonderful to look back and feel the positive feelings that were obscured by the BIG and IMMEDIATE feelings of anxiety, confusion, and overload while it was actually happening.

I watch the DVD. Every few minutes I take an orange quarter and hold it up to my nose.

Citrus. The scent of Jessa.

Open File: C:\My Files\Jessa\kiss.avi (Date 10/12/10, running time: 2.5 seconds)

Jessa nods. I kiss her. I pull away.

"Was that okay?" I say.

Jessa pulls me in for another kiss. "Better than okay." She smiles.

Close File.

Happiness. Gratitude. Amazement. Connection. I allow the feelings to surface and let myself feel them fully.

It's a lame myth that people with Asperger's syndrome are robots with no feelings. We just access emotions differently, and maybe at a different time than expected.

Like me. Right now. Close eyes. Picture Jessa's face. Smile.

I know that one kiss in the grand scheme of the world is inconsequential. I have been trained to keep my perceptions in perspective. "A computer glitch is not catastrophic." "A social embarrassment is not the end of the world." "Cursing at my mother will not make her stop loving me." (Although there are consequences unpleasant enough to keep me from repeating that mistake. . . .)

But sometimes, maybe it's okay to lose perspective? Because when something this amazing happens, it feels as if everything is right with the world. With me.

Even nongenius me has this capacity? Who would have guessed?

$(N + J) + K = j^{\text{infinite}}$

where N = Nathaniel

J = Jessa

K = one kiss

Summed up, it equals joy to the infinite power. Pure, incalculable joy.

As I watch *The Amazing Race*, I eat the orange, pulling the interior out from the peel and slowly savoring each bite. The leftover peels look like smiles.

Sweet.

CHAPTER TWENTY-THREE
THE BAT MITZVAH

"Come on up, birthday girl!" Jessa shouts into the microphone. A teenage girl, Jessa's cousin Claudia, jumps up onto the stage assisted by some people in the front row.

It is Saturday night. Jessa, Cooper, Logan, and I are already on the stage. We have just played our four-song set. The people in the banquet hall have been dancing and cheering loudly; and when Claudia joins Jessa at the mike, the cheering gets even louder.

There are a *lot* of people at this bat mitzvah.

And many sensory assaults. The noise. The necktie I have to wear. The disco ball hanging from the ceiling that sends laserlike beams of light directly into my eyes when it spins.

I am working hard not to get agitated.

Jessa gives us a cue to play a tune we had practiced specifically for this event. Jessa and her cousin share the microphone and sing "*Hava nagila, hava nagila. . . .* !" The crowd forms a giant circle, the guests placing their arms on one another's shoulders, and starts moving counterclockwise. Legs kick, people sing, the circle rotates. I recognize Jessa's older sister, Jade, and her mother, of course. Oh, there's cousin Sam. We've exchanged e-mail messages, and it turns out he likes *The Amazing Race,* too! We plan to get together soon.

I spot my friend Molly in the circle. She is wearing a dress and girl shoes. I have never seen her without horse riding boots or bowling shoes. She looks as if she is having trouble keeping up with the whole circle dance thing. But she is hanging in there.

I am very glad I am playing keyboard. If I were inserted into that circle, I would most likely lose the beat, trip over my feet, and topple everyone over like dominoes.

I shake that image from my brain and finish playing the song. Next up? The "Happy Birthday" song. Everyone serenades Claudia, who is waving to people, her long, wavy dark hair swinging down her back. That is all I can see: her back view. And the hundreds of heads in the audience.

The birthday song is over.

Claudia hops off the stage into the crowd, which has de-circled and clumped together again.

Our gig is done. The disc jockey is supposed to take over next.

The crowd quiets down. Where is the deejay?

A man with curly hair and a kippah pinned to his hair races up the side-stage steps. He motions to our band members to come over to him. Jessa sticks the microphone back into its stand, Logan emerges from behind his drums, and Cooper carries his guitar toward the man. So I go over too.

"The deejay got a flat tire," the man says. "His equipment's already set up here, thank goodness; but he won't get here for another ten minutes."

"Uncle David," Jessa says, "what can we do to help?"

Nothing, I think. I am sweaty, uncomfortable, and starting to feel suffocated by my tie and the perfumey, heavy air in the room.

"Could you guys play another song, just so everybody doesn't have to stand and wait?" Uncle David asks.

"No problem," Jessa tells him. Her uncle thanks us and leaves the stage.

Cooper, Logan, and I look at Jessa.

"Problem," Cooper says. "We don't have any more songs."

"We'll just have to play one over again," Jessa says. She and Logan and Cooper start debating which song would be the least redundant when I hear something.

"Did you hear that?" I interrupt.

"Hear what?" Cooper says. "What, Bat Ears?"

Okay, so my hearing is a bit sensitive to sounds others might not notice. Like one girl's voice in a large crowd.

"Algebra!" she yells louder.

What???????

"'Get Your Algebra On!'" shouts a different voice. It's Claudia, the bat mitzvah girl, this time.

"I sent my cousin Claudia the link to YouTube," Jessa says, "just so she could enjoy our music before her big day."

"Al-ge-bra!" a small group of girls begins chanting. "Al-ge-bra!"

Jessa walks over to the microphone and turns it back on.

"Our band has been testing out a new sound," Jessa announces. The audience goes quiet. "We put it on You-Tube recently," she continues. "Um, how many of you have seen it?"

Hands go up throughout the crowd. Lots of hands.

"Holy crud," Logan says. "We've gone viral."

"I told everybody about your video!" Claudia shouts. "We want to hear it, right, guys?"

A cheer comes out of most of the teens, boys and girls. The older ones—aunts, uncles, grandparents, the rabbi—do not cheer. Either they do not wish to hear our song or they do not watch YouTube.

"Bat mitzvah girl's special request!" Jessa yells into the microphone. She turns and hisses, "*Guys! Get ready—we're doing the algebra song.*"

We scramble to our places.

"Everybody, get ready to get your algebra on!" Jessa's fist pumps and gives us our cue.

It comes easily—the music—due to our having practiced it over and over for the video. Jessa remembers most of the lyrics (she does skip the word *Oh*) and, unbelievably, the young people in the room go crazy. They're dancing, jumping up and down, and screaming some of the lyrics right along with us.

"All you math haters, watch while I attack the FOIL method!"

"First, Out, In, and Last!"

"Get your algebra on!"

Cooper is going all guitar god, posing and joining Jessa at the mike and falling down on his knees. He sounds great. Logan is drumming the beat with an occasional stick toss and catch.

I am playing keyboard like normal. Standing, pressing keys ... I am supposed to be rocking out somehow. I think it is enough that I'm making it through this live performance without losing it.

The song comes to an end just as the deejay arrives. Everybody is clapping and yelling—some idiot holds up a lighter with a flame—and Jessa says into the microphone, "Thank you very much; you've all been great." Her voice sounds a bit hoarse. "Congratulations, Claudia! We are Igneous Rock: Logan Finley on drums, Nathaniel Clark on keyboard, and Cooper Owens on guitar. And I'm Jessa Rose, Claudia's cousin; and now it's time to party with DJ Crispy!"

DJ Crispy comes on the stage; and as we're heading off toward a door next to the stage, he says, "Yo. You guys are gonna be a hard act to follow. I caught your last tune, and they were going crazy."

The door leads to a room with some chairs, a table with bottles of water, and a large platter of pastries on it. When Cooper, Logan, Jessa, and I all are inside, Cooper shuts the door.

Ahhhhhhh ... relief.

The noise from the banquet hall is muffled, and an open window is letting in fresh, cool air. We each sit in a chair and go for the water. It's quiet as we rehydrate and catch our breaths.

I lean back and look at the ceiling, which has a pattern of tessellating hexagons. This reminds me of a geometric proof involving a bisected hexagon prism, and I picture the steps of the proof. Sides and angles and corollaries and . . .

Open File: C:\My Files\geometry_library.avi (Date: 2/5/99)

"Geometric polygons," I call out.

"Uh—please raise your hand and wait for me to call on you, Nathaniel," the lady says. *How does she know my name? Oh, I'm wearing a name tag.*

"So, children," the lady says, "what are these shapes I am holding up?"

The other three-year-olds participating in our library's Winter Art Workshop are silent. I have my hand in the air.

"Nathaniel?" the lady says.

"Geometric polygons," I repeat.

"Yes, thank you, uh, we also call them a triangle and a square," the lady says. "We will be cutting out these shapes for the snowman's nose and hat. For the body we will use one, two, *three* circles. Yes, Nathaniel?"

"You can figure out the circumference of those circles using $2 \pi r$. Do you have a ruler?"

"Today we are making snowmen," the library lady says firmly.

"Now, everyone take some scissors and cut on the dotted lines on your papers, like this."

She demonstrates. The other children begin snipping away. I am motionless. I have not mastered scissors skills, and I see a pile of glue sticks on the table. I will not touch the ooey glue.

Really, what's the point? I do not get "arts" or "crafts." I would much rather calculate the areas of the shapes, anyway.

Close File.

"What?" I say. Cooper is shaking me, his hand on my shoulder.

"Nathaniel," he says. "We're talking to you."

I blink.

"Weird," Logan says. "It's like he's either in or out. On or off. Here or . . . not here."

"Okay, okay," I say, irritated. "I'm like a binary code; I get it."

Logan's face turns as red as his hair.

"I don't get it," he says. "Did I say something wrong?"

Jessa is explaining the zero-one options of binary code to Logan—(*she's so pretty talking computers*)—when the door opens.

Jessa's mom, Sharon, and her uncle David come in. While the door is open I can hear music and singing. The door shuts. I am glad I am in here and not out there.

"Great job, guys!" Uncle David says. He walks

around and hands us each a fifty-dollar bill.

"Excuse me," I say. "This is too much money. We are supposed to get one-half of this."

Jessa's uncle laughs.

"Talented and honest," he says. "There's no mistake. You all deserve it. You came through for my Claudia and helped make her day extra-special."

Sharon has gone over to Jessa. She gives her daughter a loud kiss on the top of her head.

"Mom!" Jessa says. "You'll mess up my hair."

"You look fine," her mother says. "Boys, I know your parents are picking you up soon, but I have to warn you. There is a line forming outside the door to this room."

Huh?

"What kind of line?" Jessa says. "Mom, what are you talking about?"

"I know!" Cooper jumps up. "They're waiting for our autographs." He must have eaten a pastry, because when he jumps up, crumbs fall from his lap onto the floor.

Well, if he's eating.... I get up and take a chocolate doughnut and a bunch of napkins. The doughnut tastes amazing.

"Cooper, check your ego." Jessa laughs. "They are not waiting for our autographs."

"Actually," her mother says, "they are."

I stop chewing. A bit of doughnut gets caught in my throat, and I start coughing and gagging. *Can't. Get. Oxygen.*

Sharon runs over and whacks me on the back three times. It works. I can breathe again. Jessa's mother hands me a new bottle of water and some more napkins.

"Are you okay?" she asks. When I nod affirmatively, she leans down to whisper something in my ear.

"Then you might want to wipe your face," she says, so quiet no one else can hear. "You've got chocolate all over it."

I use a napkin on my face.

"Let's go greet our fans!" Cooper says. He looks at us with a huge grin. "Are you ready to be rock stars?"

No. I am ready to go home.

But Uncle David opens the door. Girls are screaming.

"You can come in to meet the band," he says, cupping his hands to make his voice travel loudly. "One person at a time. Just one at a time."

A girl steps into the room holding a pink pen and the pink bat mitzvah program. I had been handed a copy when I'd first entered the banquet hall. That seemed like a long time ago.

Cooper takes her pen and dramatically signs his name. He hands the program paper back to the girl, who moves on to Jessa. Then Logan. Then me.

"I can't believe I'm this close to you." The girl giggles. I am bewildered, but I sign my name in a free space near the bottom. As I hand it back, the girl squeals.

"You are such a rock star!"

I look down at my hands. My thumb has a little ink smudge on it.

I am such a rock star?

Apparently, I have no choice.

A new girl has entered the room. She doesn't approach any of us individually. Instead, she says, "Hi! I'm Emily Erin!" She's very spirited when she speaks. "I'm a cheerleader! At Sandy Creek Middle School!"

That explains it.

"Our team," she continues, "would like to use 'Get Your Algebra On!' for background music for our half-time dance routine! Is that okay? Can we?"

"It's okay with me," Cooper says quickly. "If you tell me when your next home game is."

"What Cooper means," Jessa speaks up, "is of course you can use our song, and we'd ALL enjoy seeing it used in a routine. Right, guys?"

"Yeah, sure," Logan and I say. I don't see what the big deal is; it's fine with me.

"Yay!" Emily! Erin! does a little jump-and-arm movement. "Thank you! Go, Chipmunks!"

Emily! Erin! leaves.

Jessa gets up, goes over to Cooper, and smacks him on the upper arm.

"Don't be a pig," she says. "Treat our fans with respect."

"But Jessa," Cooper whines, "they're *cheerleaders*."

I have an unwanted visual of chipmunks with pom-poms. I really don't feel right. I look down and notice little bits of napkin on my pants and on the floor around my chair. I have been shredding napkins without real-izing it.

"Next!" Jessa's uncle yells. And another girl walks in. I sigh and look up.

It's Molly. With a pink pen and a pink program. She walks over to me first.

"Can I have your autograph?" she asks.

"Molly, it's me. Nathaniel."

"I know who you are, silly." Molly pushes the paper toward me on the table and gives me the pen. "Write 'To Molly, From Nathaniel.'"

I write 'To Molly, From Nathaniel.' I notice there is something printed on the pen. CLAUDIA'S BAT MITZVAH! They must be souvenir pens.

"Alex and I are leaving," Molly says in her rushed, excited voice. "I made it for one hour and forty-three minutes. That's my personal party record! I liked your algebra song, even though I'm only in pre-algebra."

I'm weirded out. Molly is out of context here. She belongs in the bowling alley, and I am thrown off by her chatter.

"Did you know," I say, "that the Arabic people made algebra famous in 800 AD?"

"Hey! I'm half Jordanian!" Molly exclaims. "That's neat—there's Arabian math and Arabian horses!"

And she skips off to get signatures from Jessa and Logan. When she reaches Cooper, he says something to her.

"Sorry," she says, shaking her curls. "I already have a boyfriend."

She skips out the doorway with her program in hand.

"Why are all the cute ones taken?" Cooper moans dramatically. Then he adds, "Sorry, sorry, I'll be good from now on."

"You'd better," Jessa says. "This is a band, not a match-making service. Get girls on your own time."

"So much for the rock-and-roll lifestyle." Cooper sighs.

"Nathaniel, dude, are you okay?" Logan says suddenly.

I had not realized that I had taken even more napkins and ripped them into little polygons.

"Are we done?" I say. My voice is shaky and shrill

and is coming from an unsteady place. *I do not want to have a panic attack; I will not have a panic attack . . .*

I am having a panic attack. My hyperventilating breaths cause a few napkin shreds to flutter off my pants to the floor. As a fresh gust of anxiety blizzards around me, inside me, I jump up from the chair and bolt out the door.

CHAPTER TWENTY-FOUR
EQUATION CELEBRATION

I push my way through the people—girls in line, older people dancing, a man with a walker, my mother—as I head toward the red Exit sign.

My mother? I look back, but she's disappeared.

I go out the exit door. I am in the front lobby. It is mostly empty, thank goodness. I lean against a wall and pant for air.

"Nathaniel." My mother comes through the door, followed closely by Jessa. "My car's right outside, sweetie. I told you I'd be here to pick you up at seven."

I glance at my watch. 7:03 p.m. My breathing is calmer now; my heart is no longer racing. I still feel a little dizzy and nauseous.

"I'll be okay," I say. *I'll be okay, okay, okay.*

"Andrea?" Jessa says to my mom. "The whole event

went amazingly well. This . . ."—she waves toward me—
". . . just happened a couple of minutes ago. Before
you take Nathaniel home, can I talk to him for a
minute?"

"Of course," my mom says. She stands there.
Silence.

"Oh!" my mother says. "Alone! I'll wait in the car."
And she's out the main entrance and into the dusk.

"Nathaniel," Jessa says.

"What?" I notice a few white papers on my legs, and
I feel something crinkly inside my left sock. A napkin
shred. *Itchy.*

I have not spoken to Jessa one-on-one since The
Kissing. I cannot look at her now.

"Everything's okay," she says. "You were amazing. We
did amazing. Just go home and feel good. No worries."

"Yes, well, I do not think I am cut out to be a rock
star," I admit.

"Rock star, schmock star," Jessa says. "You're someone way more special. You're Nathaniel."

Her words are nice, and I lift my head to look at her.
Then something strikes me.

"'Schmock star'?" I say. "What the heck is a 'schmock star'?"

"It's just a saying." Jessa starts giggling. "Like 'diet,
schmiet,' or—"

"Jessa Schmessa?" I say. "Rose Schmose?" I do not quite get the joke, but saying the words gets me cracking up, too.

"Oh, shush up, Schmathaniel." Jessa has to stop laughing long enough to spit that one out. "Can I please have a hug before you go?"

She holds her arms out toward me, and I walk into them. I wrap my arms around her, and we stand there in the lobby like that for eleven seconds.

When we step back, I see that Jessa is smiling. I feel happy too.

"Good night!" Jessa says. "I've got to go back in. I think I hear the 'Funky Chicken.'"

As I open the passenger side door to get inside the car, my mother says, "Is there something going on with you and Jessa that I should know about?"

I sit, adjust the seat all the way back for maximum leg room, and buckle myself in.

"Something, schmomething," I say. "We are just good friends."

"Uh-huh," my mother mutters. We pull out of the parking lot, and I *finally* get to fish that napkin piece out of my sock.

Open File: C:\My Files\Jessa_sock.avi (Date 1/11/04)
My mother and I are visiting her friend Sharon. I am playing

Go Fish with Jessa and Jade.

"Nathaniel, do you have any threes?" asks Jade.

"What?" I am having trouble concentrating. My socks are too tight, and the toe part keeps annoying me.

"Threes?" Jade repeats.

"You know," Miss Sharon says, "I just bought Jade these great socks. They are soft with no seams. Show everyone, Jade."

Jade sticks out her feet and wiggles them.

"I noticed Nathaniel fidgeting with his," Miss Sharon tells my mother, "so you might want to try this brand."

"Will you, Mom?" I say. "Buy them for me?" Anything to end this torture.

"Of course," my mother says.

"Thanks, Mom." I feel a little less squirmy knowing that my sock problem will be taken care of. "I love you, Mom."

"I love you, Mom, too," Jessa says. She's always competing with me. "I love you so much."

"Well, I love my mom infinity to the infinitieth power," I retort.

"I love mine that, plus one," Jessa says.

"Yeah, well, plus two!" I say.

"Whoever says that kids with Asperger's aren't loving doesn't have a kid with Asperger's," my mother says.

"Amen to that," Miss Sharon says.

Before anyone says "plus three," Jade says loudly, "Do you have any threes or *not*?"

"Go fish," I say. "Jessa, do you have any eights?"

Ha! **She does, and I win the game.**
Close File.

The next day is Sunday. My father had a last-minute, "very lucrative" business trip out of state. So I get to enjoy a rare, quiet Sunday at home. I am drawn like a magnet to those unsolved math problems. I spend the day immersed in theoretical math research, taking a break only to do my daily walk. I need to wear a lined coat now, and the fallen leaves crunch under my feet.

People rave about New England's autumn foliage. I just find it makes my walks noisier. Next time I will carry an iPod. When I get back home, I grab a little bottle of apple cider and a cider doughnut.

"Going back up to my room," I inform my mother, who is balancing her checkbook. "If you need help with that, I can look at it later."

"Thanks," she mumbles. "Where did that six come from? Did I forget to carry the two?" More mumbles.

Up in my room, I realize I have not checked my e-mail since before the bat mitzvah. Last night I'd gone straight to bed, and this morning, I'd gone straight to mathematics.

I chug the cider, watching the new mail pop up, and take a bite of doughnut.

Then I almost choke.

Among the return addresses is one I have not seen before. It is a man's name followed by MIT.edu. A very well-known and respected mathematician's name! Followed by MIT.edu! The subject: P = NP.

I force myself to swallow; then I open the e-mail.

Massachusetts Institute of Technology
Department of Mathematics
Dear Mr. Nathaniel Clark,
My colleagues and I were intrigued by your work on P = NP. Although we came to the conclusion that your technique would not be sufficient to resolve that particular problem, we are quite interested in the Clarkization process.

I do not know if you are currently enrolled in a graduate program, but we would like to extend an offer to you to study at our institution. I would be delighted to act as your adviser under the auspices of both the Department of Mathematics and the Department of Computer Science.

Thank you for your consideration,

When I read his name again, followed by a long string of letters and awards, I go numb. Any rational thoughts I have fall out of my working brain as if through the Sieve of Eratosthenes, leaving behind only three letters of the alphabet. *MIT*.

I stumble down the stairs into the kitchen. I place

a printout of the e-mail smack on top of my mother's financial chaos.

"What's this?" my mother says, picking it up to read it.

"MIT," I say.

"What? P = NP? What are they talking about?" my mother says. "Clarkization? Nathaniel, what does it mean?"

"It means they want me," I say, still stunned. "*They* want *me*. MIT!"

"Do *you* want them?" My mother puts down the paper and looks at me.

I take exactly two seconds to decide.

"Yes!" I shout. "Final answer!"

"All right," says my mother. "You're going to MIT."

"I'm going to MIT," I repeat, tasting the words and finding them delicious.

"You can explain all this mathlish stuff to me later," my mother says. "First you need to call your father." She gives me a kiss and leaves the room.

I leave a message on his voicemail. I do not do well on the phone.

"Good news. 'Bye."

Then I try my grandma. More voicemail.

"Grandma! Great news! Call me! Your grandson! You know, Nathaniel. Right. So call me!"

Off.

I really despise speaking on the phone.

It's a good thing that MIT did not phone to tell me the news. I would have made them think they had extended an offer to a babbling idiot instead of a . . . instead of a . . .

Open File: C:\My Files\genius\second_time.avi (Date 2/22/99)
"What is he, some kind of genius?" the cashier in the checkout line asks.
Close File.

Open File: C:\MyFiles\genius\retarded.avi (Date 5/15/03)
"If he's such a genius, why can't he tie his own shoes?" my father said.
Forward
I walk into the living room.
"Technically," I say, "I'm not a genius."
I hold up the book I've been reading: *Help! My Child Is Gifted!* **I'd taken it off my mother's library pile.**
"It says in here," I tell my father, "that a genius is a person who has accomplished something outstanding with his or her talents."
Forward
"I haven't done anything exceptional that makes an impact on the world," I say. "So I am not a genius."
"You've got chocolate all over your face." My father shakes his head. "You look like an idiot."
Close File.

I slowly walk over to the front-hall mirror and look at my reflection. First I wipe the doughnut crumbs off my face. Then I see myself start to grin.

I was seven years old when I learned I was not a genius. A long, long, lifetime ago, it feels like.

But now . . . ?

Could it be . . . ?

I run down a mental checklist.

Very high IQ? Check!

My grin grows bigger.

Accomplished something outstanding? How about receiving a personal invitation to pursue my original, self-named problem-solving technique in a graduate program at a highly prestigious university? Check!

Contributing something to the world? I wrote the lyrics to songs that may make people hate and fear math and science a little less . . . (and dance more?). With just one video completed, our band has already succeeded in making people happy and educated. Mathemusicians! Check!

Check.

Check.

Check.

I have met the requirements. I've done it! It's finally true!

I am ready—and qualified—to say the words out

loud for the first time:

"I am a genius!" *I'm a genius!!!!!!* "Nathaniel Gideon Clark is officially a genius!"

The reflection in the mirror grins huge.

N does equal *G*.

N = G

Yes!

CHAPTER TWENTY-FIVE
RISKS AND REWARDS

I have officially been a genius now for three weeks and four days. I am at my desk, but, uncharacteristically, I am not using my computer. I am working slowly and carefully, unused to ballpoint pen and traditional forms.

My fingers need a break. I curl them from the pen and flex them. My knuckles crack. I am finally almost finished. I place the pen down next to the paper on which I was handwriting. I feel a bit **OLDE–FASHIONED** for a moment. *Moment over.*

I cannot help but glance over at my computer screen. Another e-mail from MIT.edu! An e-mail from MIT.edu!!!

<Open>
Dear Nathaniel G. Clark,

Congratulations on your acceptance as a commuting student to the Massachusetts Institute of Technology's Commuter Graduate Program at the School of Mathematics and Computer Science.

You will be receiving a packet with further information via Express Mail (tracking no. 2001A459S7324R) within the week. Welcome to the MIT community, Nathaniel G. Clark.

Woohoo!

<Forward> to Mom.

I wait as the e-mail message travels from my room to my mother's home office.

5 . . . 4 . . . 3 . . . 2 . . .

I open my bedroom door, and my mother races in.

"It's official?" She gasps.

"It's official," I confirm. "You will be driving me to the train station three mornings a week. And picking me up there three times a week."

"It will be worth every mile." My mother pulls me into a hug.

"Which will be two point three miles times two each day, which adds up to thirteen point eight miles each week, which will total, factoring in national holidays and vacation days . . . "

"Worth. Every. Mile," my mother interrupts. "If you promise you will *not* quiz me on math problems in the car. Promise? Good."

She is hugging me again so my mouth is muffled in her hair, and I can only say "Mrf."

When she lets go, I pick a hair out of my teeth. *Yecch. Blachh ...*

"I want to see it again." My mother bounces—literally, she bounces—over to my desk. She scans the screen.

"Looks even better over here," she says.

"That's because of the higher resolution," I say. "Your monitor is getting old."

"I meant because I'm here with *you*," she clarifies. "What's this?"

My mother is pointing to the paper on the desk next to my computer.

"It's an application," I say. "I was just finishing it."

"I thought you were finished with all the requirements for MIT," she says.

"I am." I walk over to the desk and hand her the paper.

"'Application for Stop and Shop, Inc.,'" my mother reads aloud.

"See," I say. I'm the one who is bouncing up and down now. "Look, right there."

"'Position applied for ... cashier/clerk, part-time,'" my mother reads. *Cashier! Clerk! Part-time!*

"My birthday is coming up," I remind her. "I'll

be fifteen years old and eligible to work at the supermarket!"

"Honey, I am so proud of you," my mother says. "I can't wait to be a customer in your line."

"Remember to bring your supersaver card," I say. "And hand me any coupons you have first."

I visualize myself scanning items and adding totals (including tax) as fast as the register.

"I'll have nine months before school starts," I say. "That should give me enough time to become Employee of the Month."

There is just one more thing to do before this all can come true.

Nathaniel Gideon Clark, I write where it says SIGNATURE.

"I'll drop it off tomorrow, if that's okay with you," I say to my mother.

"Sure," she says. "I'm going to go grill some steaks. We deserve to celebrate."

"T-bone steaks were on sale until yesterday, for four dollars and ninety-nine cents per pound," I say. "A real deal, especially with your supersaver card."

"That's why I bought them," my mother says and leaves the room muttering, "You're not the *only* smart person in this family."

"I heard that!" I yell.

"I wanted you to!" she yells back.

I click the ballpoint pen closed and gently place the application in a waterproof folder. I sit down at my computer. I will type in my daily journal until it is time for dinner.

> **Daily Journal, Entry #61**
> **Applied for cashier.**
> **Accepted at MIT.**
> **I had a good day.**
> *<Save>*

I have no idea why my journal writings keep coming out in haiku form. I do not even like poetry. But I do like steak. I close my file and head downstairs.

After a delicious steak dinner I head back upstairs. I immediately go to check my e-mail. I have received a new e-mail from Jessa's cousin Sam.

> **Nathaniel,**
> **I hope you are ready for our Risk match tomorrow, because I am prepared for world domination. Bring your mad skills, because it's on!**
> **Sam**
> ***Open File: C:\My Files\Sam_phone.avi (Date 11/11/10)***
> **"Hey Nathaniel, it's Sam, Jessa's cousin," the voice on the other end**

of the phone says. I knew it could not be someone I knew very well because I have made it clear how difficult it is for me to converse on the telephone.

"Sam," I say, "it's Nathaniel."

"Yeah, I know," Sam says. "Jessa says you like Risk. So do I. Want to come over next week and play a game? You can check out our new house."

"Sure," I say. "Okay."

"Cool, I'll e-mail you, and we can pick a day and time," says Sam. "But I have to warn you. Be very afraid. I am a genius at Risk."

"Uh, well, you be afraid, too," I say, "because I am a genius. At being a genius."

I say good-bye and punch a button.

"Yo! Nathaniel!" I hear a teeny voice as I am setting down the phone on the counter. I jump. I pick the phone back up.

"Yes?" I say into it.

"I think you hit the wrong thing," Sam tells me. "You didn't hang up." Stupid.

"Sorry," I say. "I didn't say I was a genius at everything."

Just before I press the Off button—the correct one—I hear Sam respond, "Nobody is, buddy. Nobody is."

Close File.

I have been Googling "Risk tips and techniques" for a while—(okay, for hours)—when my mother knocks on the door.

"Nathaniel, it's one o'clock in the morning."

"I'm in the middle of something," I say.

"Turn off the computer, please," Mom says.

"But . . . " I keep typing. I don't want to—can't seem to—stop.

"It's bedtime," my mom says loudly. "You need to turn off the computer and go to sleep."

I almost pitch a fit, but I remember the house rules. No complaining when computer time is over or . . . no computer.

I save everything and shut down the computer.

I swivel around in my chair and face my mom.

"Honey," she says, "you might still be a little manic. That happens when your meds get adjusted."

"A little hypomania isn't a bad thing," I protest.

"A little sleep is a better thing," Mom says. "Do you need help with your pj's and toothbrushing?"

"What?" I'm outraged. "I am mere weeks away from being fifteen years old!"

"Exactly," my mother says. "You do not need my help. Go. To. Bed."

"Fine." I stomp toward the bathroom. Behind every child genius is a child genius's mother telling him to go to bed.

CHAPTER TWENTY-SIX
PEEPS

"And that's a wrap," Cooper announces.

Silence.

"I think I might cry," Jessa says.

"I'm really gonna miss you guys," Logan says.

I don't say anything. I have a strange lump lodged in my throat.

"Oh, come on, everybody," Cooper says. "We'll play together again."

"When?" Logan asks from behind his drum set. "It's December, so the holidays are coming up."

"Yeah, my family's going on a cruise for two weeks around Christmas," Cooper says. "Fa-la-la fake family cheer and fake snow on the Oahu Deck."

"Hanukkah has started already," Jessa says. "It's so early this year. I have to be home every evening in time to light the candles."

"And get eight days of presents," says Cooper.

"Okay, I *want* to be home every evening," says Jessa. "Last night I got a faux fur coat."

We boys don't comment. Clothing for a gift? *Yuck.*

"Happy Hanukkah," I say. Logan and Cooper echo me.

"Thank you." Jessa smiles. "So, after Christmas there's New Year's and . . . oh . . . I have news. I got the lead role in our school musical. I'll be really busy through March with rehearsals and memorizing and stuff."

"Well . . ." Logan sighs. "We'll buy tickets and go see your performance." Cooper and I nod.

"How about Easter break?" Cooper brightens up. "It's not like we'll be hunting for eggs or anything."

"I'm going to a Christian fitness camp," Logan says. "Where Easter is about our souls and bodies, not chocolate."

"That could be fun," Jessa says.

"Yeah, I've already joined the Y and had my work-out equipment orientation."

"Good for you," Jessa says.

"Yeah, you'll have stronger muscles," Cooper says. "You'll kill on the drums."

"And lose weight," I say, trying to be supportive, too. *Silence.*

"Well, if any of us is missing Igneous Rock, we can always watch YouTube," Cooper reminds us.

"Yeah," Logan says.

"That's true," I say.

"And with our new Facebook page, we can keep in touch with each other and with our fans," Jessa says. "Thanks to Cooper, multimedia master."

"Speaking of media," Cooper says, "let's go to the rec room for our final band meeting. I've got updates. And food."

In the past few weeks, we have added to our You-Tube repertoire: "Chemistry: Don't Let It Blow Up on You," "Geometry Punk," and "Physix Musix."

Ridiculous titles (not my idea) but good tunes.

When I reach the rec room, I see a bag of chips, a bowl of candy, a plate of cookies, and Cooper's girlfriend.

"Hi!" she says, bouncing up from her chair. "I baked these cookies! Eat up while they're still warm!"

"Thank you, Emily Erin," we all say, and help ourselves.

While I had been having a panic attack at Jessa's cousin's bat mitzvah, Cooper had hunted down Emily! Erin! to apologize for his earlier "cheer-leering" during autographs. Apparently, Emily! Erin! had not been offended and had given Cooper her cell phone number.

A few texts . . . and they've been going out ever since.

"Going out"—what exactly does that mean? I'll have to post the question (anonymously) on an Aspie teens site Cooper told me about.

"Media update," Cooper says. "We now have one hundred and thirty-one 'friends' on Facebook, and our YouTube influence is spreading every day. Here's just one of the messages we've gotten.

"'Hi, Iggies!'" he reads. (People have shortened our band name from Igneous Rock. I am now an Iggie.) "'My chem teacher assigned our class to watch your YouTube tunes. Thanks for making chem seem less horrible, and I got a ninety-eight percent on my elements quiz! Eli.'"

"So make sure you check out our site, 'cause the compliments keep rolling in," Cooper finishes.

"Yeah, though you hafta weed through all the 'We heart Nathaniel' ones," Logan says.

It is so embarrassing. Girls who don't know me like me. That's because they don't know me.

Jessa leans over.

"Want another cookie?" She smiles, passing me a chocolate chip one. Jessa and I are doing well continuing our friendship. Mostly we just keep in touch online. She sends me humorous YouTube links, and I rate them from one (dud) to ten (fall over laughing).

In my world of so many variables, I am almost certain Jessa will remain a constant.

"Our keyboardist/lyricist/heartthrob will be at MIT starting . . . when?" Cooper looks at me.

"Heartthrob/*genius*," I correct him. "But do not fear, I shall remain humble and . . ."

"Starting *when*?" Cooper asks again.

"Monday, August twenty-third," I say. "At eight forty-five a.m."

"My camp ends on Friday the thirteenth!" Logan says.

"Spooky," says Cooper, causing Emily Erin to giggle.

"We can get together during the week in between," Jessa says. "Agreed?"

"Agreed!" we all respond.

"Igneous Rock lives on!" Cooper shouts. "Whoo!"

"Technically," I say, "it cannot *live* on. Minerals are not alive."

I do not know who starts the food fight, but my face is the first one to be nailed with a candy called a marshmallow PEEP.

After that, everybody and everything is fair game. Except the cookies. We all respect the cookies. Emily Erin can bake as well as cheer.

When we're worn out, Cooper, Logan, Jessa, and I clean up the mess. Emily Erin had to go, so it is just us.

Sprees for Peace. Igneous Rock.

"You've got PEEPS in your hair," Jessa says to me, and runs her fingers through it. I relax and close my eyes while she cleans me up with a paper towel.

Cooper and Logan are looking at us.

"What?" Jessa and I say at the same time.

"Is there something you two aren't telling us?" Cooper says, his eyes going squinty.

"Something, schmomething," I say. Jessa snorts.

"Igneous Rocks!" Jessa yells, and everyone's attention is back where it should be. On the four of us, all now shouting, "Igneous Rocks!"

Yep. These are my people. My peeps.

Ha.

NGC + peeps = ☺

Formulas will always be my friends. Just not my only ones.

I grin.

It occurs to me that I have many reasons to smile. I am having fun. I am a genius. I have a loyal bowling buddy and a graduate assistantship. Jessa is smiling back at me. There are only *six* years and three weeks left until I am eligible for *The Amazing Race*. And maybe, just maybe, by then I will have discovered that P = NP. Or not.

Whichever it is, I'm okay with that. In fact, I'd

venture to say N = OK, where N = Nathaniel and OK = okay (not Oklahoma).

OK. Sometimes even much more than okay. And sometimes much less. But it averages out to be okay.

Normal? No. Typical? Not even close. But on the spectrum of life, for me to be okay is pretty darn amazing.

The End

(Except for one more thing . . .)

THE ASPERGER'S AMAZING RACE

	1	2	3	4	5	6	7	8	9	10	11
Nathaniel Clark	2nd	1st	2nd	6th	4th	4th	1st	4th	2nd	3rd	1st
Thomas Jefferson	3rd	2nd	3rd	5th	5th	2nd	2nd	3rd	1st	1st	2nd
Marie Curie	5th	5th	4th	2nd	6th	1st	5th	2nd	3rd	2nd	3rd
Albert Einstein	1st	3rd	1st	1st	1st	3rd	4th	1st	4th		
Temple Grandin	10th	7th	5th	3rd	2nd	5th	3rd	5th			
Spock	8th	6th	6th	4th	3rd	6th					
Charles Schultz	6th	9th[2]	7th	7th	7th						
Molly	4th	8th	8th[3]	8th							
Andy Warhol	9th	4th	9th								
Jane Austen	7th	10th									
Isaac Newton	11th[1]										

By Nathaniel Gideon Clark

NOTE 1: Isaac Newton was disqualified for refusing to leave his house.

NOTE 2: Charles Schultz initially arrived 7th but left his *Peanuts* comic at the detour and incurred a 30-minute penalty.

NOTE 3: Molly initially arrived 5th but incurred a 30-minute penalty for improper use of transportation: riding on a horse instead of walking.

JENNIFER ROY

LEG 1: USA   FRANCE
New York City, New York, United States (Central Park) (Starting Line)
New York City, New York (Newark Liberty International Airport) to Paris, France (Charles de Gaulle International Airport)
Paris, France (Arc de Triomphe)
Paris, France (Avenue des Champs-Élysées)
Paris, France (Hôtel de Ville)
Paris, France (Eiffel Tower)
Paris, France (La Grande Arche)

LEG 2: FRANCE   GERMANY
Paris, France (La Défense)
Paris, France (Gare Montparnasse) to Frankfurt, Germany (Frankfurt Hauptbahnhof)
Frankfurt, Germany (Frankfurter Paulskirche)
Düsseldorf, Germany (Rheinturm)
Düsseldorf, Germany (Goethe-Institut)

LEG 3: GERMANY   IRELAND
Düsseldorf, Germany (The Colorium)
Düsseldorf, Germany (Düsseldorf International Airport) to Shannon, Ireland (Shannon Airport)
Shannon, Ireland (Shannon bus station) to Galway, Ireland (Bus Éireann)
Galway, Ireland (Eyre Square)
Galway, Ireland (River Corrib)
Galway, Ireland (Galway City Museum)

LEG 4: IRELAND   CHINA
Galway, Ireland (Galway Airport) to Beijing, China (Beijing Capital International Airport)
Beijing, China (Tiananmen Square)

Beijing, China (Temple of Heaven)
Beijing, China (Xidan)
Beijing, China (Dongdan)

LEG 5: CHINA ARGENTINA
Beijing, China (Beijing Metro station)
Beijing, China (Beijing Capital International Airport) to Santiago,
Argentina (Comodoro Arturo Merino Benítez International Airport)
Santiago, Argentina (Paseo Bulnes car park)
Mendoza, Argentina (Puente Viejo, "old bridge")

LEG 6: ARGENTINA SWEDEN
Mendoza, Argentina (Governor Francisco Gabrielli International
Airport) to Santiago, Argentina (Comodoro Arturo Merino Benítez
International Airport)
Santiago, Argentina (Comodoro Arturo Merino Benítez International
Airport) to Stockholm, Sweden (Stockholm-Arlanda Airport)
Stockholm, Sweden (Bogs Gard Farm)
Stockholm, Sweden (Tivoli Gröna Lund)
Stockholm, Sweden (Stockholm-Arlanda Airport)

LEG 7: SWEDEN THE NETHERLANDS
Stockholm, Sweden (Stockholm-Arlanda Airport) to Amsterdam, the
Netherlands (Amsterdam Airport Schiphol)
Amsterdam, the Netherlands (Amsterdam Centraal railway station)
Amsterdam, the Netherlands (Melkmeisjesbrug)
Amsterdam, the Netherlands (Amsterdam Centraal railway station)
Ransdorp, the Netherlands (Rural Village Field)

LEG 8: THE NETHERLANDS RUSSIA
Amsterdam, the Netherlands (Amsterdam Airport Schiphol) to Moscow,
Russia (Domodedovo International Airport)

Moscow, Russia (Novodevichy Convent)
Moscow, Russia (Ostankino Palace)
Moscow, Russia (Sokolniki Park)

LEG 9: RUSSIA
Moscow, Russia (OKB Sukhoi)
Moscow, Russia (Triumph Palace)
Tula, Russia (Yasnaya Polyana)
Tula, Russia (Arsenal Stadium)
Moscow, Russia (North River Terminal)

LEG 10: RUSSIA   JAPAN
Moscow, Russia (Domodedovo International Airport) to Tokyo, Japan
(Tokyo Narita International Airport)
Tokyo, Japan (Ochanomizu University) (This was originally a Detour,
but since all teams chose the same option, the other detour option was
edited out of the show)
Tokyo, Japan (Tokyo National Museum)
Tokyo, Japan (Olympic Stadium)
Tokyo, Japan (Tokyo University of the Arts)

LEG 11: JAPAN   USA
Tokyo, Japan (Bunkyo Civic Center)
Tokyo, Japan (Tokyo Imperial Palace)
Tokyo, Japan (Tokyo Narita International Airport) to Los Angeles,
California, United States (Los Angeles International Airport)
Los Angeles, California (Kodak Theatre)
Los Angeles, California (Los Angeles Memorial Coliseum)
Anaheim, California (Disneyland—Main Entrance) (Finish Line)

ACKNOWLEDGMENTS

Thanks to my editor, Margery Cuyler, and to my agent, Alyssa Eisner Henkin, for being so incredible.

Also, thank you to Brian Buerkle, Sean Crowley, and Michelle Bisson at Marshall Cavendish. And thank you to Jessica Olivo at Trident Media Group.

I am eternally grateful to my family: my twin sister and best friend, Julia DeVillers; my invaluable mother, Robin Rozines; my awesome husband, Greg (who is *nothing* like the father in this book!); and my amazing eight-year-old son, Adam.

Thanks to my extended family members, including Jack DeVillers (Adam's BFF); Quinn DeVillers (world's best niece); David DeVillers; David, Peter, and Ethan, and the Vermont Roys; Sylvia Rozines and all the Rozines cousins; the Perkins clan; the Rudnicks; and our Fresh Air daughter, Destiny Blackmond Robinson.

Thank you to Robbin and Chris Rybitski (your family rocks); and Matthew (mathmentor genius) and Bill Babbitt. I am truly blessed with the friendships of the Aibel family, the Aldous family, the Tellstone-Sheehans, the Gillespies, the Akawis, and the Barrs.

Much appreciation goes to the Asperger's, gifted, and homeschooling communities! And to Doctors Jung, Meyer, and Malin.

Finally, THANK YOU to the public and private school teachers, librarians, parents, and students who have invited me for visits, written letters, and supported *Yellow Star*. You have made me one grateful, humbled, and happy author!